STUMP SPEECH MURDER

A Pamela Barnes Acoustic Mystery

by

Patricia Rockwell

For information, email **Cozy Cat Press**, cozycatpress@aol.com or visit our website at: www.cozycatpress.com

COZY CAT
P R E S S

ISBN: 978-0-9848402-3-6
Printed in the United States of America

Cover design by Scott Saunders of Design 7 Studio, www.design7studio.com

10 9 8 7 6 5 4 3 2 1

Dedicated to my Dad, whose journalism career must have been the source of my love of writing.

Chapter One

". . . and that's what my campaign is all about! Our community is filled with brilliant minds—minds I'd like to put to work to solve the problems that Mayor Brewster and the present administration have let fester over the years. Maybe they hoped that those problems would just solve themselves! Or that you, the voters, would forget that those problems existed. But, my fellow citizens of Reardon, the way to solve our city's problems is not to ignore them! No, it's to tackle them head on! And that's what I intend to do!

"There's no reason that Reardon should be experiencing the economic downturn that it is. We have excellent natural resources, a willing workforce, and business leaders who are daring and bold. We should be soaring! But Mayor Brewster is simply not far-sighted enough to take the initiative and bring our community into the next century."

"How long do you think this speech will last?" Pamela Barnes asked her colleague and friend Joan Bentley. It was a hot August day in the Southern college town of Reardon, and Pamela was hoping not to have to spend her entire afternoon standing outside in the blazing sun listening to a stump speech.

"Shh!" responded Joan, with her slightly grande dame manner. "He's discussing his education plan now." Joan leaned forward in rapt attention. *You'd think she was listening to some Hollywood movie star*, thought Pamela. The speaker was James Grant, a local lawyer and Joan's friend and fellow member of the Human Subjects' Committee at Grace University where they both worked. She'd been hearing Joan sing the praises of young Mr. Grant for almost a year now. How he willingly sacrificed time from his very busy schedule to serve on the Human Subjects' Committee. How he genuinely cared about education issues even though he himself was not an educator or even had any children in the local schools. How he intended to run for mayor and clean up corruption in city government. Needless to say, Joan had been smitten by the young man's plans—and also probably by his down-to-earth good looks. When James Grant had asked Joan to work on his campaign, she had jumped in with both feet. Unfortunately for Pamela, Joan kept trying to drag Pamela along. But she was just not fascinated by local politics.

". . . Our present mayor has neglected his duties. He has focused his attention on personal gain and not on bringing prosperity to Reardon. I will change all that!"

She glanced at her wristwatch. Oh, no. It was after five. Her husband, Rocky, would be wondering where she was. He probably had dinner started—no doubt something delicious. She always relished the fact that she was married to a marvelous gourmet cook who seemed to love to do the one thing she thoroughly despised—cooking. What amazing dish would he concoct tonight?

". . . and with your help, I know we can win this election!" intoned the young politician, brushing a lock of his wavy brown hair from his forehead.

"Pamela," Joan said, nudging her. "The rally is over. Let's get going."

"Oh, wonderful!" responded Pamela with relief. "Wasn't that a fine speech?" She wanted Joan to see that she'd been paying attention.

"Of course it was," noted Joan, seeming annoyed.

"What's wrong?" asked Pamela.

"There's hardly anyone here from the media," Joan replied, looking around the rally spot which was situated in an open, grassy area in McPherson Park. From here, Pamela could see James Grant surrounded by various young campaign workers. Most of these individuals were handing out flyers and posters to attendees. At a distance, Pamela could see a local news van had arrived and she recognized television news anchor, Ginger Cooper, and her entourage heading over to Grant and his group.

"There is now," she said. "Look! It's that Ginger Cooper from WRER."

"Finally," sighed Joan. "Come on, I'll introduce you to James."

"Oh, Joan," said Pamela, hesitating. "It's getting late. He looks very busy. There are so many people around. And . . . and . . . the media are going to want to interview him. He won't want to meet me . . . ."

"It'll just take a second," Joan snapped, grabbing Pamela by her sleeve and heading towards the dashing young politician who was standing under a large shade tree, surrounded by well-wishers and supporters.

"James," gushed Joan, shoving Pamela in front of him. "This is my friend and colleague Pamela Barnes—also from the Psychology Department. Pamela, James Grant—the next mayor of Reardon!"

"Um, how do you do?" said Pamela, thrusting her hand out which James Grant took and shook warmly.

"Ah, yes!" he replied. "Dr. Barnes! The acoustics detective! I've read about your work. You've been very helpful to our local police on a number of cases."

"Just a few, actually," mumbled a blushing Pamela.

"I'm trying to get Pamela involved in your campaign, James," added Joan with a smile.

"That would be wonderful!" he said. "We can always use the help of clever, resourceful women like . . . the two of you. Can't we, Martin?" He called out towards a handsome black man in a fashionable summer suit standing a few feet away, clipboard in hand. The man acknowledged Grant with a raised hand and then disappeared into a group of campaign volunteers who engulfed him.

"Mr. Grant!" called out the news reporter, Ginger Cooper, as she enveloped the politician with her team of technicians. Suddenly, a sound boom was hanging between Pamela and the young man and a cameraman had pushed in front of her and was already filming. "Mr. Grant!" continued Ginger Cooper, "can we get your reactions to the latest *Reardon Advocate* poll that indicates your numbers running slightly ahead of Mayor Brewster's?"

Joan grabbed Pamela's arm and pulled her back, so the reporter could have easier access to the politician. Joan and Pamela watched for a while and listened intently to the interview in progress. Looking across an expanse of green grass and shade trees towards the parking lot, Pamela saw a group of men disembark from a large black van. The men headed towards them and Pamela recognized the man in the lead as Hap Brewster, Reardon's long-time mayor. The other men in tow, she assumed, were Brewster's assistants.

"Oh, no," whispered Joan as she also saw them. "Here comes trouble. Every time James gets some media coverage, that Brewster fellow has to butt in."

"He is the mayor," noted Pamela. "He's running for re-election. It's not strange that he'd be trying to get his message out."

"Pamela, are you nuts?" Joan cringed. "He has no message except, 'vote for me or suffer the consequences'."

"You make him sound like a Mafia don."

"That's fairly close to the truth," said Joan. Harold "Hap" Brewster, a robust and virile-looking bald man with piercing blue eyes, walked purposefully towards the reporter. Following him were two other men. The older one was grey-haired, overweight, with a long sharp nose. He looked like he could and would eat anyone who got in his way. The third man was younger, probably in his late thirties. He was dressed more casually than the other two, wearing a blue shirt and chinos and his tie was undone and partially hanging around his neck.

"Here comes Don Hap now," said Joan, nudging Pamela, as the three men approached the small crowd gathered around candidate Grant and the TV reporter.

"Miss Cooper!" called out Hap Brewster. "I see you're again wasting your time interviewing this upstart. I thought I told you what such foolishness could do to your career."

"Mayor," retorted Ginger Cooper loudly, her amber-flecked eyes flashing, "as an unbiased journalist, I consider it my job to get each candidate's positions on the issues. I've interviewed you and I will interview you again. I'm merely gathering information. I'm doing my job."

"If your job includes wasting your time," pronounced Brewster's rotund assistant, "Miss Cooper, then you are certainly doing it well." He gave an almost imperceptible bow and a smug smile in the reporter's direction.

"Who's that?" Pamela asked Joan.

"The grey-haired guy is Brewster's second in command—Victor Baines."

"And the young one?"

"I think that's Kevin Sturges," said Joan. "He's the Communications Director."

"He's not doing much communicating," replied Pamela.

"He's more a behind-the-scenes kind of guy," said Joan, "as I've heard Martin tell it."

Pamela knew that Martin was Martin Dobbs, the African-American man now busily directing James's volunteers. Joan had told her that Dobbs was James Grant's friend, law partner, and most recently—campaign manager. She could see him still standing several feet behind James, watching the interview taking place. Pamela had gathered from Joan that Dobbs was a jack-of-all-trades. As Pamela glanced from one campaign camp to another, it was immediately obvious which group had the more experienced, well-honed team. Hap Brewster had a professional entourage of seasoned adults—probably all well paid–working for him. James Grant had his best friend, Martin Dobbs, a handful of young, eager Grace University students, and a few stalwart faculty volunteers like Joan, assisting him. A rag-tag bunch if ever there was one.

"Mr. Baines," noted Ginger Cooper, ever the professional, to Hap Brewster's second-in-command, "if you will have your

. . . candidate . . . wait just a moment until I've finished speaking with Mr. Grant, I would be delighted to get Mr. Brewster's comments too." Pamela detected that Ginger Cooper took some pleasure in referring to the reigning mayor as a candidate. She could almost see Brewster bristle when Ginger called him "Mr." instead of "Mayor." Ginger Cooper seemed oblivious to Brewster's reaction. No doubt, any type of dissention between the two men vying for the top job in their community would make for good footage—and probably get Ginger the lead story on the local evening news.

Hap Brewster huffed and ruffled his jacket like a rooster shaking his feathers among a gaggle of hens. Campaign Manager Victor Baines leaned over and whispered in the mayor's ear. Communications Director Kevin Sturges appeared to be observing the interplay between his two superiors, glancing back and forth from them to Ginger Cooper, who was just completing her interview of James Grant. Catching the reporter's eye, Sturges beckoned with a slight movement of his index finger. Ginger rolled up the cord of her hand-held microphone and, with a motion to her sound man and videographer, headed over to the Brewster group under a leafy elm tree about twenty yards from where Pamela and Joan stood.

"Joan," Pamela said, "I'm going to head on home. Rocky is probably wondering where I am."

"That's fine, Pamela," replied Joan, listening but watching the candidate. "But, before you go, just tell me you'll join James's team."

"I don't know, Joan," Pamela replied, hesitantly. "I'm not really into politics. I've got so much on my plate right now."

"Pamela Barnes," sniffed Joan, turning to her friend, "you don't have any more on your plate than I have on mine! And if I can help in this campaign, which will ultimately benefit every resident of this town—particularly residents with a vested interest in education, and that includes you—then so can you! You owe it to yourself—and your students—to help get this young man elected."

That was a little much, thought Pamela. She doubted that she owed it to her students to get involved in some local election. What she owed her students was to be the best teacher she could be. But Joan was probably right that Pamela should show some civic pride–and young James Grant seemed like a bright, honest, well-educated individual–a far cry from his opponent incumbent mayor Hap Brewster who basically owned their pretty little town along with his cronies. What harm could there be in helping out a bit with his campaign? And—it might even be fun. She always had fun when she and Joan plotted together—and they could surely plot ways to get this young leader elected—or at least they could plot how they could assist him.

"Okay, Joan," she agreed. "I'll help with the campaign."

"Wonderful!" cried Joan. "When the two of us put our heads together—how can he lose?"

Pamela felt a certain amount of buoyancy as she drove home. She'd never been involved in a political campaign before and there really was an element of excitement about it all. Of course, Rocky would probably think it all too demanding and he'd no doubt nix the whole idea, but—oh, well—she'd deal with that later. As she drove into her driveway and parked her little blue Honda in her garage, she noticed that her big, burly husband was standing at the kitchen door waiting for her, wooden spoon in hand and a large white butcher's apron tied around his waist.

"I'm late, I know," she said apologetically, as she grabbed her books and class papers, and slid past him into their homey kitchen.

"No problemo," he responded. "How did you enjoy the rally? Did you get to carry a poster on a big stick?"

"Nope," she said. "I just listened to his speech and to Joan's play-by-play. I tell you I think she's enamored of the man. She dragged me up to meet him afterwards."

"So, is he John Edwards cute?" asked her husband with a scowl.

"Not as cute as you," she replied, wrapping her arms around him from behind as he stirred something on the stove that smelled really wonderful—and spicy. "But he does have John Edwards's hair. Joan guilted me into working with her on the campaign," she said cringing, waiting for a negative response.

"Hmm," he said flippantly. "Sounds like fun."

"You think?" she asked. "It might mean getting involved with the local political mafia. That Hap Brewster really has a bunch of scary-looking minions."

"So you make a few posters and hand out some flyers—no big deal."

"I'm glad you understand," she said. "What is that yummy-smelling sauce you're making?"

"Velvet Cheese."

"How much time do I have before it's ready?"

"Just change and get back here—maybe ten minutes."

She headed into the bedroom, stripping herself of high heels and panty hose, and flinging on a worn out pair of sweat pants and slippers. She turned on the bedroom television set and listened as she made herself comfortable.

"Local mayoral candidate—James Grant–," said a WRER anchor at his desk, as a video clip from the afternoon's rally appeared on the screen. *That was quick*, she thought. It hadn't even been an hour since she'd seen the reporter conduct this interview. Pamela bent in close to the screen to see if she could see either herself or Joan, but only Ginger Cooper and James Grant were visible. The screen switched suddenly back to the studio anchor.

"Shortly after this interview was taped, local mayoral candidate James Grant was arrested."

Pamela gasped.

"Sources indicate that Grant's wife Stacy called 911 at 5:28 p.m., telling the operator that her husband was trying to break into their house. When police arrived at the Grant home shortly afterwards, they found James Grant standing over his wife's dead body."

"Oh my God!" she screamed.

Rocky bolted from the kitchen into the bedroom.

"What's wrong?"

"The candidate! James Grant! I went to his rally!"

"So? What happened?"

"They just arrested him for killing his wife."

Chapter Two

Much later that night, Pamela and Rocky sat in their bed munching on popcorn. Their small, white poodle, Candide, was scrunched between them where he could quickly nibble up any falling kernels.

"I just can't get over it," Pamela said for about the third time. "I just met the man this afternoon. He seemed so pleasant—so friendly."

"Pleasant friendly people have been known to kill people," noted her husband, a handful of popcorn halfway to his mouth.

"Like who?"

He shrugged. "They said Lizzie Borden was well liked in her community."

"But, Rocky," she moaned, turning to her mate, "why would he do this? I mean, forget the horror of the crime itself—bashing his wife over the head with a big brass candlestick, according to one source. I mean, why would he do anything to jeopardize his chances of winning the election?"

"Yeah," replied Rocky, scratching his face, now rough with a full-day's growth of beard, "a murder rap sort of puts the kibosh on his political aspirations."

"If he was having problems with his wife," she continued, "why not seek counseling or—at worse—file for divorce? I mean, other candidates have gotten divorces and still managed to get elected. It doesn't have the stigma today that it once did."

"I don't know, Pammie," he scowled. "Maybe it was some long-brewing battle between them. Maybe he just snapped all of a sudden."

"But, why?" she demanded. "What would be so horrible that it would cause him to freak out and kill her?"

"Maybe he came home and found her with another man," he suggested, surreptitiously tossing a kernel towards the foot of the bed where Candide bounded after it with the speed and intensity of a big jungle tiger leaping upon prey.

"That's impossible!" she cried.

"Why?" he asked. "You've been involved in enough police investigations to know that people often behave in strange ways."

"I know," she agreed, pulling the bowl away from him and digging for the few remaining salty kernels at the bottom. "But that's not what I mean. I mean it's impossible because if he found his wife with another man, why didn't he kill the man? Why kill the wife?"

"Hey!" he pouted. "Men are strange."

"Tell me about it," she said, nudging him. "And besides, if there was another man in the house, you'd think the media would be reporting that."

"Why?"

"'Cause the media always assume the juiciest of explanations," she argued. "Surely, that's the first thing that the reporter imagined. That Ginger Cooper was probably all over the police with questions about possible other men."

"So," he said, "if you don't think there's another man, what do you think? Why did this seemingly nice guy—with everything going for him—suddenly lose it? Up and kill his wife and then make absolutely no attempt to cover his tracks?"

"That's the more important question," she responded, nodding.

"What's the more important question?" Rocky made one of his annoyed huffing sounds. Candide, now having given up on getting any more popcorn, snuggled up to his master and licked his fuzzy face in his most ingratiating, doggy fashion. "Nope, buddy. Not popping any more tonight."

"Why would he do something like this that would so obviously ruin his chances to win the election?" She held the popcorn bowl on her lap and drummed her fingers on its edge.

"Maybe the wife wanted him to drop out of the race," offered Rocky suddenly, propping himself up on an elbow. Candide plopped off of Rocky's shoulder and scampered to the foot of the bed in case more treats were in the offing.

"So what if she did?" she asked. "He could just say no. Couples disagree. I don't smash a candlestick on your head when you and I don't see eye to eye."

"Yet," said Rocky.

"What does that mean?" she scoffed. "I'm a very gentle person."

"A very gentle, headstrong person," he corrected.

"We frequently agree to disagree," she noted in an even, well modulated voice.

"As do most couples," he allowed, nodding.

"Just my point," she said. Silent, then Rocky and Pamela both stared ahead, apparently deep in thought. Candide looked back and forth from master to mistress. Neither seemed to be making a move towards the kitchen. With a small, infinitesimal doggie shrug and a delicate moan, he lay down at the foot of the bed where he maintained an eagle eye on his owners for any possible change in their behavior.

"What about your friend Joan?" asked Rocky after a while.

"What about her?"

"She's the one who dragged you into this political campaign business," he said. "What does she say about this guy getting arrested for murder?"

"I don't know," she replied, her tone changing abruptly. "I'm surprised I haven't heard from her, come to think of it. She'll probably be horrified. She really likes him. Actually, she thinks the sun rises and sets on him."

"It sounds like she has a crush on him," he suggested.

"At times," agreed Pamela, "I think the same thing. Joan is usually so sensible about things, although she does have a bit of a wild side."

"What do you mean by that?" he asked, askance.

"Rocky," sneered Pamela, "she is a widow. I mean, she's single and she certainly hasn't been a recluse. Although, she's very discreet." She batted and rolled her eyes in his direction.

"You mean, her students don't know anything about her amorous activities."

"Correct," said Pamela, giggling. "At least, not that I know. I have to admire her. I mean, if I were in her shoes—and I'm really glad I'm not in her shoes—but if I were, I would wish that I had her adventuresome spirit." She leaned over and nuzzled her husband's cheek.

"My dear," said Rocky, winding his arm behind his wife's back and burying his nose in her neck, "you are quite adventuresome enough for me!" The increasing movement between the couple caused the bundle of fluff at the foot of the bed to leap up and join in the activity. Not exactly what Rocky apparently had in mind. "Shoo! Go back to Westphalia, silly dog! Your timing is not good!"

"Just be mindful of yourself, Mr. Barnes," chastised Pamela.

"Oh?"

"I wouldn't want to have to kill you," she replied, popping a finger against his nose.

"Oh, babe," he answered, "for what I have in mind, there will be no motive for murder in our house tonight."

Chapter Three

Pamela caught sight of Joan Bentley the next morning as she was making her daily pass around Blake Hall looking for a parking space. Unfortunately, Pamela had arrived too late to secure a spot in the small departmental lot next to the imposing two-story brick structure, so she was resigned to driving in circles around the block until a space opened up in the lot—or more likely—a parallel spot cleared on the street. As she drove slowly around and around, keeping an eagle eye peeled for the slightest movement of a front tire on one of the parked vehicles, she noticed Joan's red Taurus passing in the other direction. Joan had obviously arrived as late as she had, which was unusual for her early-rising friend. She reasoned that Joan had probably positioned herself in front of her home television set to get the latest report on the arrest of James Grant and couldn't drag herself away until the last minute. From the brief glimpse Pamela got of Joan as she whizzed by, Joan did not look happy.

Great, thought Pamela, *we'll both be stuck out here looking for parking spaces and we'll be lucky if we find spots and get inside in time for our first classes. I was hoping I'd have an opportunity to find out what she knows about the arrest of this James Grant.* As she whined to herself, a student driver pulled his jalopy out from a tight parking spot near the corner, screeching his tires in defiance of the close quarters of his car's position, and zoomed down the street. Pamela pulled up directly to the car in front of the empty spot, much more cautiously than the previous resident had left—because she'd had her share of parallel parking mishaps—and expertly maneuvered her little Civic into the empty spot. *A perfect location*, she said to herself, right under a tree to keep her car cool during what would likely prove to be a typically hot August day.

As she extricated herself and all of her daily paraphernalia (purse, thermos, lunch sack, books, papers, grade book, clipboard) from the front seat of her car, and headed across the street to the main entrance of Blake Hall, she saw Joan walking quickly towards her from the opposite direction.

"I cannot believe I got a space on my first time around!" announced Joan, joining Pamela as the two women walked up the flight of cement steps that led to the big, white, double doors marking the main entrance to the Psychology Department at Grace University.

"I suppose you're late," noted Pamela, "because you were watching the local news."

"Tell me about it," said Joan, wiping her hand over her forehead. Pamela didn't know if the perspiration there was from worry or the weather.

"My God, Joan," continued Pamela, as the two professors walked through the large lobby and headed left down the main hallway. "What happened? Your candidate was arrested for murder!"

"My candidate!" cried Joan, grabbing her briefcase in both hands and heaving it up into her arms. "If I remember correctly, you joined James's team yesterday. Didn't you?"

"Yes," agreed Pamela, scrunching up her forehead as they entered the Psychology Department's main office immediately on their right. "But I'm assuming his candidacy is over now. I mean, he's in jail!"

Joan moved to the wall of faculty mailboxes on the side wall of the office. She bent over and peeked into a small cubby and removed a batch of envelopes, flyers, and cards. "It must be a mistake," she whispered to Pamela. "It just must be. I'm sure they'll straighten everything out."

"Joan," countered Pamela, retrieving her own mail from her box. "His wife is dead. That's not something you 'straighten out.'" Joan gave her a sign to keep quiet and the women silently exited the main office and headed down the hallway and up a staircase at the far end.

"You mean to tell me," asked Pamela, "that you think there's been some sort of mistake?"

"Obviously," said Joan with a shrug, "it's not a mistake about his wife being dead. But surely, it's a mistake that he's being blamed for it."

"What makes you say that?"

"Because I've gotten to know James, Pamela," she insisted. "I know him and I know he could never do something like that!" They arrived at Joan's office as she scrounged around in her jacket pocket and brought out her key chain and quickly unlocked her office door. She stomped into her office, placing her items neatly in a pile on the top of her desk. She quickly moved to her window and readjusted the blinds so that a blast of morning sunlight changed the color and the atmosphere from gloomy to bright.

"Sometimes we think we know someone," said Pamela, plopping herself down on Joan's neat leather sofa. Joan busied herself behind her desk with a small pitcher of water that she carefully poured into five or six planters on her desk and bookshelves.

"Pamela," said Joan, taking her seat behind her desk, and assuming her professorial voice, "Believe me, I'm as shocked as you. But, this just must be some sort of mistake. I tell you I know James. I've gotten to know him. After all, we worked together on that Human Subjects' sub-committee for over a year. I feel like he's a really close friend—or a brother."

"Not a boyfriend?" Pamela continued to clutch her belongings.

"What?" Joan gasped. "What are you suggesting? James is married."

"Not anymore," said Pamela, grimly.

"That's disgusting, Pamela," said Joan. "He's more than twenty years my junior."

"So?"

"Listen," said Joan, scooting closer to her desk and leaning forward. "You know—and I know—that I enjoy an invigorating relationship with a man from time to time. But— I am not a home wrecker. And more important, James Grant is a loyal husband."

"And you know that for a fact?" asked Pamela, leaning forward, her chin resting on her stack of books and papers.

"Where are you getting these ideas, Pamela?"

"I don't know," said Pamela, somewhat deflated now. "It just seemed to me that you were so wrapped up in all of this political campaign business, I began to wonder if there wasn't something more to it than just your enthusiasm for Mr. Grant's platform."

"That's ridiculous!" barked Joan. "What do you take me for?"

"I take you for a normal person, Joan," said Pamela in a tense whisper. "You wouldn't be the first person to get involved in a political campaign because they were enamored of the candidate. Haven't you heard of Monica Lewinsky?"

"I'm not enamored of James," Joan shot back, her neat white hairdo glistening in the sunbeams from outside. "I'm enamored of his ideas and his plans."

"That's all I wanted to know," said Pamela. "But, if that should change . . ."

"It won't," Joan snapped.

There was a long silence as the two women both took deep breaths and slumped in their seats. Pamela deposited her belongings on the sofa next to her. She reached over to Joan's office door and tapped it shut. *Too little, too late*, she thought. If any students had been in the hallway outside, they had probably already gotten an earful.

"Anyway," began Pamela, looking carefully at Joan's face. She had never seen Joan cry—ever. Joan was the most stoic of all her friends and colleagues. She remained calm during any and all crises. Now, Pamela thought she observed the beginning of a tear—not an actual tear, but just the beginning of one in Joan's eye.

"Can we talk about this?" asked Pamela.

Joan, suddenly pulled herself together and, sitting up straight behind her desk, started to put things away in drawers in a pitiful attempt to make her desktop neat.

"Joan?"

"What?" Joan stopped her busy work and glared at Pamela.

"What do you know about what happened? Do you know anything?" Her eyes pleaded with Joan.

"I don't know any more than you do. I probably know less. I didn't even hear about the arrest until late last night because I came back here after the rally to work on that article I have to get done for *Ed Psych Reports*. So when I did hear about it, it was so late that I didn't . . . couldn't call you . . . or anyone to find out anything. So all I know is what they reported on WRER."

"They're saying the police found him standing over the body."

"I know. Evidently, she had called 911 to report that someone was trying to break in."

"No," disagreed Pamela. "I thought the news said she reported to 911 that her husband was trying to break in."

"That doesn't make sense," argued Joan, now doodling on her blotter with a pencil. "Why would James need to break into his own house?"

"I'm sure that's what they said on the news."

"I'm sure he has a key to his own home. Why would he break in?"

"Maybe she locked him out with a chain lock or a dead bolt," suggested Pamela, leaning back onto Joan's sofa and crossing her legs.

"Why?"

"Rocky says that maybe they were having marital difficulties. Maybe he came home because he suspected something, broke in, and found her with a lover."

"I haven't heard even a hint of anything like that," mused Joan, "and I've been at the campaign headquarters fairly regularly over the last few weeks."

"If they were having difficulties," offered Pamela, "you might assume that they'd try to keep it quiet so that the media wouldn't get wind of it."

"I don't know."

"Have you ever seen his wife?" asked Pamela.

"Stacy," said Joan. "I've not only seen her, I've met her—and she's lovely. Well, she was lovely. She worked for the DA's office."

"And they seemed okay?"

"I guess," responded Joan. "I mean, they weren't billing and cooing all the time. When she showed up at campaign headquarters, she'd only stay a while."

"Do they have children?"

"No," replied Joan. "I think they'd only been married a few years."

"Hmm," mumbled Pamela. "You wouldn't think they'd be having trouble so soon, would you?"

"The only possibility I can think of is that maybe the campaign itself might have taken a toll. You know, on the marriage. James spent almost every single minute of the day on that campaign. If Stacy was prone to being resentful, I guess she'd have the campaign to resent."

"But her being resentful," said Pamela, "is backwards."

"How so, Sherlock?" asked Joan with a snide leer over her glasses.

"I mean, it would seem Stacy would be the one to have a motive to murder James, not James having a motive to murder Stacy."

"That does seem more logical," considered Joan, leaning back in her big leather desk chair, "if anything about any of this were logical."

A knock on Joan's office door shook the two friends from their contemplation. Pamela rose and opened the door.

"Dr. Bentley," said a scruffy-looking young man standing respectfully at the entrance. "You said in class yesterday that we should stop by and have you look over our rough drafts of our research papers. I was wondering if you'd mind taking a look at mine?"

Joan gestured for the student to enter. Realizing their private conversation was at an end for the moment, Pamela nodded farewell to Joan and headed out of the office and across the hallway to her own. As she let herself in and unloaded her own things in their proper places, she continued to mull over the strange situation. A nice young man—an ideal candidate for mayor performing well in the polls and whom Joan supported and whom she would probably support too—had suddenly, seemingly thrown away his chance at a position of leadership. He'd thrown away his chance to make real substantive change in their town by viciously killing his wife and then stupidly making no attempt to cover his tracks. Did any of this make any sense?

No, she thought, as she slid onto her comfy paisley sofa beside her window that looked out onto the campus grounds. No, none of it makes any sense at all.

Chapter Four

Pamela barely had time to open her thermos and take a few sips of one of Rocky's specialty teas, when Joan appeared at her door, breathless.

"Quick!" she waved at Pamela. "Arliss just called. She said to come right away!"

"Oh, my!" responded Pamela, setting down her cup on her end table. After quickly locking her office door, she followed Joan down the hallway. Arliss was the third member of their tight little group and she was in the last few weeks of her first pregnancy. A call from Arliss to come *immediately* must mean the baby was on the way.

The two women pattered down the stairs, their heels echoing in the old stairwell. On the main floor, they hurried towards the animal lab, of which Arliss was director, which was located at the end of a long corridor on the other side of Blake Hall's main lobby. Passing the main office, they flew past the departmental secretary, Jane Marie Mira, who was just locking the office door and putting up a sign announcing her departure for a few minutes while she made her daily foray to the administration building to pick up the Psychology Department mail.

"Dr. Barnes! Dr. Bentley!" called the young secretary. "Where are you running to?"

"It's Arliss!" responded Joan, yelling over her shoulder as she whizzed by Jane Marie.

"Is the baby coming?" asked Jane Marie, now following behind the two faculty women.

"We don't know," said Pamela, between huffs and puffs. "She just called and said to come right down to the lab!"

"Maybe she's in labor!" suggested the secretary, joining in the excitement of the chase.

As the three women reached the far end of the corridor that led to the animal lab, they came to a large, swinging, double door. A sign above announced, "Grace University Animal Psychology Laboratory." Pamela did not venture here often, but she did know that the lab had recently undergone some dramatic improvements, thanks in part to Arliss's efforts and those of her husband, Bob, who was head of the department's animal psychology sequence. Joan, being in the lead, pushed through the two doors, and the three women careened inside.

All around them were rows of cages and wire baskets and fenced areas where animals of varying types and sizes resided. The odor of the large room was definitely gamey, but not nearly as strong as Pamela had remembered it several years ago before Arliss and Bob had made the major improvements to the program. The giant room also seemed much lighter and airier as the floor to ceiling windows in the old place had been cleared and cleaned. Pamela knew that Bob had installed a new ventilation system and the entire lab shone and sparkled.

"Over here!" called a voice from the farthest end of the lab above the sounds of squeaks, cries, and chirps. The three women quickly hustled down the center aisle, past cages of birds, rodents, monkeys, dogs, cats, and various other laboratory creatures—all seemingly cheering the running women on in their own unique species' way. When the three reached the back of the lab, they saw their friend, Arliss MacGregor Goodman, bending over a medium-sized cage in the last row next to the wall. Arliss was skinny to the point of being emaciated—except for the large belly she now sported. Her mass of frizzy black hair was tied up in a loose pony tail.

"Look!" she cried to the three women. "Look at Eva!"

"Arliss!" exclaimed Joan, with a deep breath, and standing to her full height, "What's this about? We thought you were having the baby!"

"No!" replied Arliss, with a slight sheepish grin. "I'm fine."

"Your water didn't break?" asked Jane Marie, carefully.

"No!" said Arliss. "But somebody's did—so to speak. Look at Eva! She's a mother."

The three women cautiously and rather squeamishly bent over and peeked into the small wire cage where Arliss was pointing. Inside, a small white, round, furry animal was huddled in the corner on a pile of wood shavings. Underneath her, barely visible were the tiny heads of several baby creatures of the same type."

"You scared us to death, Arliss!" scolded Pamela. "We thought we'd have to deliver your baby ourselves right here on the floor of the lab."

"I'm sorry, Pam," said Arliss with a frown, then suddenly grinning, "but I just wanted you to see Eva's babies. Aren't they adorable?"

"Adorable," said Joan with a fake grin. The corners of her mouth rose abruptly and then returned to normal.

"Cute," agreed Jane Marie. "They smell a bit though."

"You don't understand," continued Arliss, waving her thin fingers frantically. "This is our first live birth in the lab in years. It's really a wonderful sign that conditions have improved dramatically for our animals. When animals can mate and produce young, it's a wonderful benefit for an academic lab—in more ways than one."

"What is it, a hamster?" asked Pamela. She peered into the cage, her nose wrinkling in response to the odor.

"Oh, no!" laughed Arliss. "Eva is a chinchilla. We named her that because she has such a beautiful and expensive fur coat. And, of course, Eddie is very doting too—he's the father. That's him—asleep in the corner over there."

"Eddie?" asked Joan, tapping a finger on the corner of her glasses.

"Like Eddie Arnold," said Arliss. "From that old television series. *Green Acres*. You know, Eva Gabor and Eddie Albert. Bob is nuts about it. This guy takes his fancy city wife to live on a farm."

"No wonder Bob likes *Green Acres*," mused Pamela, "as he owns a farm himself."

"But Bob certainly doesn't have a fancy city wife," noted Joan, giving Arliss a glance from head to toe.

It will be fun to name all five of her babies," interjected Arliss. "I may have a contest and let the students have a go at it."

"All right," said Joan, exhaling. "It's a relief, I guess, that you're fine. I mean, you are about ready to drop that Goodman kid any day now. Couldn't you have imagined what we'd think when you called and told us to rush to the lab right away?"

"I'm really sorry," replied Arliss, sucking on her lower lip and patting her large belly. "I know that when this baby is ready to make an appearance, my friends will be right there to help."

"Just think of this as a dry run," offered Jane Marie. They all laughed and carefully took turns bending over Eva to look at her five little youngsters. Eva wiggled her tiny pink nose and fluffed her fur up in a useless attempt to hide her brood from prying eyes.

"Really, Arliss," noted Joan after some minutes had passed. "My heart simply will not withstand any more excitement today."

"More excitement?" asked Arliss. "It's not even ten o'clock, Joan. What else exciting has happened today?"

"James Grant," pronounced Joan, "was arrested yesterday for killing his wife! Haven't you heard? I've been working on his campaign."

"You mean that young guy who's running against Hap Brewster?" asked Jane Marie, her large brown eyes glistening.

"Yes," agreed Pamela, as the four women now stood in the center aisle of the animal lab, their heads together. "It was on the news last night. His wife evidently called 911 to say her husband was trying to break into their house. When the police arrived a few minutes later, they found James Grant kneeling over her body."

"Oh, my god," exclaimed Arliss. "How awful!" She rubbed her stomach protectively.

"Oh, no!" cried Jane Marie with a shiver. "If he's sent to prison, that means Hap Brewster will be a shoo-in to win re-election in November."

"I know," replied Joan. "This is all simply horrible."

"Ladies," said Pamela gesturing them together into a tighter group, "of course, it's not good if Mr. Grant loses the election, but far worse is the fact that his wife is dead—and he's the primary suspect."

"*Only* suspect, don't you mean?" suggested Arliss. "I mean, if they found him standing over her body, how could they suspect anyone else?"

"How demoralizing this all is," said Jane Marie, shaking her head. "We've lived in Reardon all our lives and Hap Brewster has been mayor as long as I can remember. He and his cronies run this town. No one's ever had the courage to confront him before James Grant. I was really hoping that Mr. Grant would get elected—and maybe things would be–different."

"Different? Different how? You sound like you know more about this than we do, Jane Marie," said Pamela.

"All I know," replied Jane Marie, "is that my husband works in the oil fields and he gets an earful about local politics all the time and how the good ol' boy network affects that industry. He's also heard about the way Brewster and his gang have manipulated and controlled other local businesses. He says that if you want to succeed in Reardon you have to play ball with the Brewster crowd or you can forget it."

"So, James Grant's arrest is quite a coup for Brewster," noted Pamela, aware that the departmental secretary's longtime residence in the community gave her perspectives into local politics that Pamela didn't have—being herself a relative newcomer of only fourteen years.

"Of course!" agreed Jane Marie. "Dr. Barnes, it just makes me sick! Here I thought we finally had a chance to rid this town of its more unsavory elements—and now this man whom we all thought could be our savior goes and ruins it all for himself and everyone else!"

"That's only if he did it," argued Joan. "It all seems too pat to me. Too much like a set-up."

"Set-up? How?" asked Jane Marie.

"I mean," continued Joan, as the other women listened intently, "of all the people in the world whom Hap Brewster would probably want out of the picture, would probably want to see in jail, arrested for a crime—James Grant would be the most likely. James's arrest is Hap Brewster's fondest wish."

"It could all just be coincidence," suggested Arliss, the mother-to-be, meekly squeezing her maternity tunic.

"If it's a coincidence," said Joan, looking pointedly from one woman to the other, "then I'm a monkey's uncle."

"We have two monkeys in the lab, Joan," offered Arliss. "If you'd like to meet your nephews."

"I don't hurt pregnant women," scowled Joan in response, lifting her elbow mock-menacingly towards Arliss. "If you think about it, there's something really fishy about this—and no, Arliss–I don't want to go look at the fish in your tanks."

"Surely," said Pamela, "Hap Brewster wouldn't order Stacy Grant killed just to get rid of his political competition."

"It's possible," whispered Joan, bending her head of silver curls towards the center of the group. "But I wouldn't breathe a word of speculation on this topic if I were you. You never know who could be listening."

"About 178 ears," noted Arliss, nodding at the cages surrounding them.

"Does that include Eva's new offspring?" asked Jane Marie, changing the tenor of the conversation.

"It does!" announced Arliss. "We keep close tabs on our creatures."

"A lot better than anyone has kept tabs on our mayor and his entourage," noted Joan, as she drew them close again. "I wonder just how many local journalists he has in his pocket."

"Like Ginger Cooper?" asked Pamela. "She certainly wasn't afraid to ask James a lot of hard questions at that rally yesterday, if you noticed, Joan."

"Yes," agreed Joan, "she's a go-getter. I wonder if she was as aggressive about interviewing Brewster when he showed up yesterday? We left about that time. Remember?"

"No one is aggressive about interviewing him," said Jane Marie. "Haven't you ever noticed that? Reporters know better than to pin him down. They know what might happen to their careers—what has happened to careers—if they ask Hap Brewster anything but innocuous questions. Plus, he has that campaign manager of his—that Victor Baines—always out there clearing the way for him. He has a huge machine."

"I'm sure a far bigger machine than James Grant has," said Joan, despondently, "or had."

"Oh, Joan," said Arliss, giving a warm hug to her friend. "Don't give up. I think it's wonderful that you're trying to help make Reardon a better place. And if you say that this James Grant can do it, I believe you." She lowered her voice and dropped her head. "Maybe he was set up."

"Dr. Barnes," said Jane Marie suddenly, "I bet you can help solve this crime."

"I don't see how," replied Pamela. "The police have already made an arrest. As far as I know, they don't need anyone to listen to any recorded messages that might identify a suspect for them. That's all I've done in past cases."

"You never know," insisted Jane Marie. "You're a real detective, Dr. Barnes. If anyone can help this James Grant, if anyone can find out what really happened, and who killed his wife—assuming he didn't do it—it's you, Dr. Barnes."

"Yes . . . Dr. Barnes," chuckled Joan. "Our very own Agatha Christie. Trust me; James did not kill his wife. But because the police believe he did, they will, no doubt, make no additional effort to find the real killer. I guess that leaves you, Pamela. You'll have to find Stacy Grant's killer."

"Thanks," said Pamela without enthusiasm. She did not intend to get herself embroiled in another murder investigation. She looked back into the chinchilla cage at Eva and Eddie, snuggling up together around their new brood. "You two are so lucky you live in Green Acres," she sighed. "I'm stuck here in Reardon in the center of a big mess. I wish I could join you in there."

Chapter Five

After her morning classes, Pamela nabbed a copy of the local newspaper—the *Reardon Advocate*—from Jane Marie's desk and seated herself in the secretary's alcove where she pored over the front page story. The headline read, "Local Mayoral Candidate James Grant Arrested for Wife's Murder."

Reardon city police were called to the home of James and Stacy Grant at 110 Cornelia Blvd., yesterday at 5:36 p.m. According to city Police Chief Joseph Bellows, a 911 emergency operator directed officers to the Grant home when Mrs. Grant called 911 at 5:28 p.m., to report that her husband was attempting to break into their home.   When officers arrived, they discovered the front door open, and inside found James Grant kneeling over his wife's dead body, apparently attempting to revive her.   Officers also reported that they discovered a large, bloody brass candlestick on the ground next to the body.

Hmm, thought Pamela. *According to this report, James had apparently been trying to revive his wife.* If that was true, and it wasn't just a hoax to make himself look grief-stricken, then it implied that James entered his home and discovered his wife—already dead. *A distinct possibility*, Pamela thought. Of course, it was also possible that James left the rally yesterday, went home, got in a terrible fight with his wife— and killed her.   Then when the police arrived, he just pretended to be reviving her. Or, he could have killed her and then become genuinely remorseful and actually was trying to resuscitate her. *There were a number of possible scenarios*, she thought.

One element that seemed to hold promise for some immediate investigation, Pamela thought, was the time element. Because of the call to 911 and the almost immediate arrival of the police who had recorded the exact time of their arrival—two important pieces of information were known to the minute. Stacy Grant had called 911 at 5:28 p.m. and the police had arrived at 5:36 p.m.—only eight minutes later. How likely was it that Stacy Grant could notice her husband attempting to break into their home, call 911, and James Grant could break in, bash his wife over the head with a brass candlestick, and then attempt to revive her just as the police arrived? Could all of that have happened in the space of eight minutes? Pamela surmised that it was possible but unlikely.

"Dr. Barnes," said Jane Marie, with a startle as she noticed Pamela sitting there. She slid neatly behind her little desk in front of the only window in the room. "Were you waiting for me? I just zipped out to the restroom for a minute." She picked up a powder compact from her desk and quickly gave her nose a puff. Always neat, Jane Marie was attractive and dressed nicely, but certainly not ostentatiously. Today she had on a simple print cotton skirt and a white organza short-sleeved blouse.

"No, no!" said Pamela. "I just wanted to read this story in the *Advocate* about the murder."

"Oh, yes!" said Jane Marie. "Poor Mr. Grant! My husband had such hopes that things would improve if he were elected."

"You insinuated as much down in the lab this morning, Jane Marie," said Pamela, scooting her straight back chair closer to the secretary's desk. "You husband evidently has much to complain about with regards to the present city government."

"Oh, don't get me started, Dr. Barnes," replied the pert secretary. "According to him, there's not a business in Reardon that wouldn't rejoice if someone could defeat Hap Brewster—not anyone!"

"Really?"

"I'm not kidding, Dr. Barnes," she said, removing her flying fingers from her keyboard momentarily and leaning towards Pamela. "That man runs this town like his own private fiefdom. No one opens a business in Reardon without the approval of Hap Brewster. And believe me; you can't get his approval just by a friendly handshake."

"Can't someone report him to the Federal Trade Commission—or something?" asked Pamela.

"If anyone has tried, nothing has worked. At least, nothing has since I've lived here—and I've lived in Reardon all my life," Jane Marie whispered. Pamela wondered who might be listening.

"He doesn't seem to bother the University," mused Pamela.

"I know," agreed Jane Marie. "And we can consider ourselves lucky. I think it's just because he has no interest in Grace. There's a big separation between the school and the city—if you know what I mean."

"I do," said Pamela. It was true. Many townspeople, she knew, perceived of their local university as another world that just happened to be stuck right in the middle of their downtown area. She was quite certain that many residents of Reardon drove around the edges of the Grace campus as they went about their daily activities—avoiding and ignoring the scholarly pursuits going on within.

"But believe me," continued the secretary, her shiny dark curls bouncing as she spoke with animation and intensity, "the businessmen—and women—in Reardon are well aware of Mayor Brewster and how he controls this town. They may not personally be able to counteract his grip on the community, but I know they were all thrilled about James Grant taking him on in the upcoming election."

"So, many people in town are going to be devastated about James's arrest?"

"Yes," she said, nodding. "And totally demoralized. He was a last hope for many."

"Jane Marie, do you think Hap Brewster could have set up James for his wife's murder?"

"He would certainly have the clout to do it," suggested Jane Marie, scratching her head thoughtfully, "but I don't know if he'd have the ingenuity. It would be more like Brewster to just threaten people to vote for him or get their kneecaps smashed. A devious plot in which he kills a rival politician's wife and then manages to implicate the man in her death, seems really far-fetched—even for Hap Brewster."

"It does to me too," agreed Pamela. She leaned her elbows against the top of Jane Marie's desk, pondering the situation and rereading the front page story. "I wish I had more information. This newspaper story only provides the bare essentials."

"I can't help you there," said the brunette, shrugging and continuing her typing. Pamela realized that she had probably intruded on Jane Marie's work time and that she should get back to her own office in case students were piling up outside of her door. Although it was summer and she was only teaching two classes, she could never predict just when a student from one of her classes would show up asking for help. As it was technically during her posted office hours, she headed out of the departmental office and up to her office.

On her way down the second floor hallway, she noticed Willard Swinton's office door open. As she walked by, she saw Willard sitting alone at his desk, uncharacteristically watching his small television set, instead of being hard at work on one of his research projects. As Willard and Pamela shared similar interests in language and vocal features, they often collaborated on research. She stopped at his door.

"Watching soap operas in the middle of the afternoon?" she questioned the large black professor with a suppressed giggle.

"Pamela," he said to her, looking up from his small black and white screen that resided on top of one of his four, five-foot high filing cabinets. "I turned this on to see what the local news might be saying about James Grant's arrest."

"Do you know James?" she asked, stepping inside Willard's office. This office was an exact replica of hers, although Willard hadn't invested nearly as much time as she had in decorating his space. He did have a number of photographs of various groups to which he belonged. She knew, for instance, that in his youth, Willard had served in the Navy and was exceptionally proud of his accomplishments while he was enlisted.

"I don't know him well personally, my dear," said Willard, motioning her to take a seat in the padded straight back chair in front of his desk. "But I have certainly heard about him and everything he's been doing for Reardon. Amazing man! And, of course, I do know Martin."

"You mean, his campaign manager?"

"His campaign manager and long-time friend and law office partner. They are actually more like brothers—if such a thing can be said about a black man and a white man—but they are. Here, my dear! Look!" Willard directed Pamela's attention to the television screen. Text appeared on the screen as a recording played. "It's the 911 call from the wife. Listen."

He turned up the volume with a small remote on his desk. Pamela focused on the small screen. The picture quality was not good and the sound quality was even worse. Even so, the call from James Grant's wife to 911—although short—was riveting.

"My husband . . . outside . . . trying to . . . break in. Please help!" That was all. Almost immediately, the call ended—or the caller hung up. She couldn't tell. The audio recording continued with the voice of the 911 operator. "Ma'am . . . can you tell me your address? Ma'am, please don't answer your door. Ma'am? Ma'am?" The operator continued to attempt to make contact with the caller but the line was dead.

The television reporter then pointed out the caller's hysteria the operator's calmness. The co-anchor made a comment about the conversation between Stacy Grant and the operator, if you could call it a conversation, and then they played the recording again. Pamela listened a second time, noting the elements of the recording in which her research made her an expert—the sound of the caller's voice. As she glanced at Willard, she could tell that he had been doing the same thing and had probably listened to Stacy Grant's 911 call more than once. Finally, after they had both heard the emergency call at least a dozen times, Willard switched off his television set with his remote.

"So, Pamela," he said, looking at her with a questioning glance, "what do you make of that?"

"I'm not sure," she said hesitantly. "There's something strange about it though."

"Yes," he agreed, "but I'm not sure just what it is either." He sat quietly, looking down. His round, compact body seemed to draw together like a turtle pulling inside its shell in contemplation of its next move.

"I wish I had a copy . . . ." she said, almost to herself.

"Ah, my dear!" he interrupted her with a start, as if she'd awakened him from a daydream, then leaned over to his computer's hard drive and pressed a button which opened a drawer. Popping out a compact disk, he slid it into a paper sleeve and handed it to Pamela. "I thought you might say that, so I made you one."

"Willard," she chuckled, "you never cease to amaze me." And it was true. Saying farewell to her colleague, saluting him with the new CD in hand, she headed out his door and a few steps down the hallway to her own office. She was relieved to note that, contrary to what she had feared, no students were lined up waiting to see her. She would be able to enter and think—about a very unusual 911 call.

Chapter Six

Several students did eventually show up and Pamela helped them develop their research paper ideas. Even so, the afternoon had that lazy summer day quality. With only two classes to teach, no committees meeting to attend, and all of her research projects on hold until the fall semester when her graduate assistants would again be providing her with help, the summer seemed very much like a vacation. Pamela was able to sip her tea and listen to the 911 call made by Stacy Grant only minutes before her death. Now–later in the afternoon–she was not only able to listen to the recording, but also to look at a visual display on her computer screen of Stacy Grant's voice and the emergency operator's voice as the terse conversation progressed through the use of her acoustics analysis software. Her experienced eye traced the sharp lines of the two voices—noting the fluctuations and pauses, the variations in intensity, pitch, and other vocal phenomena. She was lost in thought as she played and re-played the brief recording.

"Pamela," called a soft voice at her door. She looked up to discover Willard standing there with another African-American man and Joan. "Pamela, I hate to disturb you."

"Oh, Willard," she replied, closing down her acoustic program and rising to greet her two colleagues and the unknown visitor. "You're not interrupting. This has actually been a very slow day . . . very few students." She smiled and motioned for the three people to enter. Joan, uncharacteristically quiet, escorted the visitor in and then turned and carefully shut the door behind her.

"Pamela," said Willard, "I'd like you to meet Martin Dobbs. Martin, my colleague Pamela Barnes." Dobbs, immediately reached out to shake Pamela's hand with both of his.

"Dr. Barnes," he greeted her. "I can't tell you how much it means to me to hear that you are interested in helping James."

Pamela looked at her two colleagues quizzically.

"Pamela," said Joan, "remember, I told you about Martin. He's James's campaign manager."

"Actually," interjected the energetic Dobbs, "not only his campaign manager, but also his business partner—and long-time, best friend. James and I were roommates in college and we've been sort of tied at the hip ever since. It sort of seemed natural that we would open our own law firm together after we both graduated from law school at the same time."

"Mr. Dobbs," Pamela said, "yes, I remember you. Actually, Joan took me to the rally in the park yesterday. I remember seeing you there. Would you like to sit down?" She gestured to the group and Dobbs and Willard immediately plopped onto Pamela's comfortable sofa and Joan took up her typical post in the straight back chair near the door. Pamela returned to her desk chair.

"I was there all right," Dobbs responded, laughing. "Wherever James goes, I go. If you must know, James was originally going to hire a campaign manager. Really! Well, I wasn't going to have that. I told him, if he had the gumption to run against Brewster—then he was getting me for a campaign manager. And, believe it or not, I think I've done a pretty good job." His cheerful, expressive face suddenly fell—in rhythm with his powerful shoulders. His eyes latched onto Pamela's like a vise. "Well, at least I thought I was doing a pretty good job until yesterday. We were ahead of Brewster in the latest poll—not much, but a little. Then it all fell apart."

"Pamela," said Joan from across the room by the door, "Martin appealed to Willard and he to me for help. You said yesterday at the rally that you were going to work on James's campaign . . . ."

"Oh, wonderful, Dr. Barnes!" interrupted Dobbs with a small bounce on the sofa cushion. "We can use all the help we can get. Of course, I didn't expect things to get so bad . . . ."

". . . and I know you'd never renege on a promise," continued Joan, pointedly at Pamela. Pamela cringed. Joan would hold her to her unenthusiastic commitment from yesterday and somehow would now force her to help this man.

"I was happy to help with Mr. Grant's campaign," said Pamela politely, "but I'm not sure there's anything I can do for him in these new circumstances . . . ."

"You mean, now that he's been arrested for murder," said Dobbs, shaking his head forlornly.

"Martin," chastised Willard. "You cannot give up."

"I agree," urged Joan, bending in towards the two men. "Surely this is all a mistake. I can't help thinking that some horrible error has been made. I told you that, Pamela."

"I wish you were right," sighed Dobbs, "but if there is some horrible mistake, I don't know what it is. Stacy was murdered—and for all intents and purposes—it certainly looks like James did it."

"It wouldn't be the first time that an innocent person was falsely accused," argued Joan, clenching her fists.

"Unfortunately, the police are convinced that James did it," said Dobbs, looking even more despondent.

"Stop it, Martin," said Willard. "I've known you for years, and I've never known you to be a defeatist."

"It's hard not to be a defeatist, Willard," said Dobbs, "when James has totally given up himself."

"What do you mean by that?" asked a riveted Pamela.

"I mean . . ." continued Dobbs, outstretching his hands in an expansive gesture. Pamela was hard pressed to say which man was more inspiring, the James Grant she had heard yesterday at the rally, or Martin Dobbs, sitting here on her couch, pleading his case. Dobbs continued, "I just spoke with

James this morning. He's so devastated about his wife's death that that's all he can think about. He seems totally oblivious to the fact that he's been arrested for her murder. Yes, he claims he's innocent, but he doesn't know who did it—and worst of all—he says he doesn't care!"

"What?" cried Joan. "I can understand how upset he'd be, but he can't just give up!"

"I know!" explained Dobbs, turning to face Joan. "And I do think he'll come around eventually, Dr. Bentley, but I don't know when. He's just been dealt a terrible blow. His own welfare—and certainly his campaign—are his last concerns!"

"He needs a good lawyer!" suggested Willard.

"He's got one!" announced Dobbs. "Me! He's my top priority. And, although I don't want to belittle the importance of the campaign—because James and I got involved in the campaign together and we both had high hopes about that—but the campaign has to take the back burner for a while because—well, face it—there is no campaign if James is convicted of Stacy's murder."

"Right," agreed Joan. "On the other hand, if—when—James is exonerated, the police will be forced to look elsewhere for her killer—and that may lead them straight to the Brewster camp."

"Don't say that too loud," noted Dobbs, waving his hands around like an old-fashioned Baptist preacher. "If it's true that the Brewster campaign had anything to do with Stacy's death, then you can never tell where they have spies." His gestures and facial expression created an impression of skullduggery and dark deeds.

"I think you're safe in my office," suggested Pamela, looking around, suddenly fearful. "And, Mrs. Grant's death may not be connected to Brewster and the election. There may be things going on that we know nothing about. But, I agree that the main concern has to be exonerating James. That may mean—as Joan implies—finding the real killer, if indeed, James is innocent."

"Anyway," continued Dobbs, "I'm going to fight for James and defend him for all I'm worth in court. I've hired an investigator too, and he's looking into many of the obvious avenues. And, of course, where the election is concerned, time is of the essence. I—we—just can't afford to let the legal system grind along at its typically slow pace. We have to find out who really killed Stacy—and we have to do it quickly. James needs everyone helping in every way possible. That's why I asked to meet you, Dr. Barnes."

"Me?" asked Pamela. Now she was curious. The eyes of everyone were fixed upon her.

"I've known Willard," continued Dobbs, "from our work together on our church Board of Directors for several years now. Joan, of course, I met a while ago when she started volunteering on James's campaign. Both of them speak glowingly about your efforts in solving a number of crimes that had puzzled the local authorities. All I'm asking, Dr. Barnes, is for your professional expertise in helping James— even if he doesn't appear to want any help at the moment. I'm sure that eventually he will come to grips with Stacy's death and will want to discover the person who is responsible."

"Mr. Dobbs," replied Pamela, leaning back in her desk chair and folding her arms. "I would certainly be willing to assist your candidate and friend in clearing his name if I could. I just don't see how my particular expertise can help in Mr. Grant's circumstances. I mean, it's not as if the police have recordings of him—or anyone—committing the crime. My expertise is basically in using acoustic technology to differentiate one human voice from another. I don't see how Mr. Grant's voice comes into play at all in this case."

"That's true," agreed Dobbs, with a quick glance at Willard, "but Willard tells me that you have gone beyond your primary research areas from time to time in your crime fighting efforts."

Pamela chuckled. "He did, did he?"

"No more than I would do, my dear," said Willard sweetly. "You are a champion of the down-trodden." His cheeks puffed out and his dimples indented.

"Willard, flattery," she said, "and all that. All right, Mr. Dobbs, what is it you want me to do?"

"Just be aware," said Dobbs. His smile vanished and he bent towards her, leaning his long, expressive fingers dramatically on his kneecaps.

"That doesn't sound too demanding," said Pamela.

"Just be aware of what's going on in the investigation," he continued, "and if you see—or hear—anything that seems even the slightest bit out of the ordinary, please let me know. And Willard and Joan, I would ask the same of the two of you. I'd like to count on you three as my faculty contingent. You three are psychologists with expertise in different areas. I'm hoping that the three of you can put your educated heads together and ferret out a clue or two that might explain what happened. Why did James get arrested for a murder he didn't commit?"

"I guess if we're going to do any ferreting, we should include our animal psychologist—Arliss?" suggested Joan.

"By all means," agreed Pamela, with a shrug. "The more, the merrier." She would obviously need all the help she could get.

Chapter Seven

"... and as he is presently in jail without chance of bail, it is the contention of our campaign that Mr. Grant should remove his name from the ballot.   After all," continued incumbent Mayor Hap Brewster, a barrage of microphones vying for attention in front of his face, "if a candidate is incapable of serving, then he has no business running." As the mayor looked directly into the nearest camera lens, several reporters peppered him with additional questions.

"He's disgusting," said Pamela to her husband as they nibbled on squares of meat and vegetables that were skewered to long pokers. A fondue pot bubbled away on a low table in the center of their living room and the couple lounged on pillows on the floor, dipping their food tidbits into the boiling liquid. They were each sipping a fruity Cabernet. "He really seems to enjoy the fact that James has been arrested." Candide remained a respectful but eager distance from the savory-smelling meat.

"It does leave him without an opponent," noted Rocky, gnawing on a large chunk of beef and several small onion pieces. Candide moaned audibly.

The local news program returned to the studio anchor who noted almost the same thing—but in much less biased terms. With James Grant in jail, unable to get released on bail, and a trial probably weeks, if not months away, it appeared that Hap Brewster would easily be re-elected in November. Even with James's recent upsurge in the polls, being arrested for murder would no doubt greatly reduce his chances of being elected.

"Can he even still run?" asked Pamela. "I mean, now that he's been arrested, that he's in jail? Is he even allowed to keep his name on the ballot?" She chewed on a crispy chunk of green pepper at the end of her fondue stick. Candide pawed the air in a not-so-subtle attempt to get her attention.

"I don't know," responded her husband. "I guess if he got on the ballot legally, he can stay there until—and unless—he's convicted. I mean, innocent until proven guilty—remember." He plucked a tiny cherry tomato from the end of his skewer and plopped it into his mouth. "Yum."

"But, Rocky," she sighed, "who's going to vote for a man arrested for murder?" He emptied the bottle of Cabernet into their wine glasses. Candide, seemingly frustrated at his efforts being ignored, eventually lay down, his tiny head placed woefully upon his front paws.

"More people than will vote for one convicted of murder," he suggested. "I don't know if the guy is better off staying in jail until after the election and hoping people vote for him out of sympathy and hatred of Brewster—or going to trial and hoping somehow he's found innocent in time enough to reclaim his good name and win the election on his own."

"How can that happen? Hap Brewster would never let it happen!" she cried, taking a swallow of her wine. "You saw him on the news just now. He's going to pound and pound about James being in jail, being arrested. He's going to make such a stink about this that I just bet they'll be forced to take James's name off the ballot."

"I don't think he can do that, Pammie," Rocky said calmly to his irate wife. "Not legally anyway."

"If there's one thing I've discovered in the last day or two," she huffed, "it's that legality is not something that stops Brewster." With that, she stuck a potato chunk on her empty skewer and poked it into the sizzling liquid. Being the foodies that they were—Pamela liked to eat as much as Rocky liked to cook—nothing was as enjoyable as a do-it-yourself type of meal like fondue. They always had fun cooking the food as they ate it—sometimes even feeding each other (and once in a great while—their dog) especially tasty morsels—and drinking lovely wines. And at times, their intimate fondue parties became even more intimate when the supplies ran out. Tonight, however, Pamela was enraged over Hap Brewster's television news conference in which he expressed his outrage over the murder of Mrs. Grant and her husband's apparent culpability.

"Whatever he can do—legally," continued Pamela, stretching out on the floor pillows, "doesn't mean that he should be doing what he's doing. Calling a press conference and then gloating—you know that's what he's doing, Rocky! Calling a press conference and dwelling on James's arrest is really slimy. An ethical politician would not be making a public statement about his opponent's personal tragedy and how it could—should–affect the race."

"Maybe not," agreed Rocky, sliding down to her level on his own set of pillows, "but, Babe, no one in this town would ever mistake Hap Brewster for an ethical politician."

"You should probably know that James Grant's campaign manager came to my office today," she whispered, as she downed the last few drops from her glass.

"What for?"

"Willard and Joan wanted me to meet him."

"How do they know him?" he asked.

"Joan met him while she was working on James's campaign. Willard knows him from their church. This man— the campaign manager—Martin Dobbs, is also James Grant's law partner and evidently now his lawyer. He came begging the three of us to help him with James' defense."

"What?" Rocky sat upright and set down his glass with a thud. Candide bolted upright. This could mean that food was on its way.

"He merely wants us to keep our eyes open and to see if we notice anything unusual. I mean, he's aware of my experiences with the local police. I guess Willard told him— or Joan did. Not sure. He's convinced that James didn't kill his wife. So are Willard and Joan. Nobody seems to think he's capable of it."

"So, why should that involve you?"

"It doesn't actually. He just wants the three of us," and here Pamela was cautious to indicate to her husband that she was just one of a group, "to be observant."

"I know you," he scowled, "and being observant is what's gotten you into a lot of trouble before."

"There were reasons then," she whined. "There were sound clues and I was able to use those clues to identify a killer. But in this situation, the police have who they believe is the killer. They don't need to identify anyone. There aren't any sound clues . . . ."

"Yet," noted Rocky.

"Probably never," she shot back. "Well, there is the 911 call, but that's of the victim . . . or supposedly the victim." She looked away from him, deep in thought. "But, even so," she said, suddenly all smiles, "all I promised the man was that, along with Willard and Joan, I would keep my eyes open."

"See to it that that's all you do," he said, pointing a finger directly in her face.

"Rocky!" she wailed. "Don't be mean!"

"I'm not being mean; I'm being protective!" Candide was now upright and leaping back and forth between Rocky and Pamela.

A telephone rang and Rocky fumbled around on the floor and finally located his cell phone.

"Yeah? Oh, Angie! Hi! Your mother and I are fonduing!" he chuckled. Pamela knew that their daughter Angela always found it amusing when her parents stretched out on the living room floor and fed each other hot pieces of meat—as she put it. He handed Pamela the phone.

"Hi, sweetie," said Pamela into the receiver.

"Hey, Mom," said her daughter. "Just calling with good news. I got a raise at work." Angela had graduated from Grace and was now working at a small non-profit organization devoted to fundraising for a children's charity. She and her boyfriend lived together in a small apartment.

"Wonderful!" said Pamela. "She got a raise!" Pamela whispered to Rocky, who gave a small fist pump. "How's Kent?"

"Don't know; haven't seen much of him this week," replied Angela. "We're starting a big campaign to raise a hundred thousand dollars for our kids. I'm going to be really busy with it. I may even have to do some traveling."

"That sounds like fun," replied her mother. Pamela knew that Angie was not terribly adventurous and that traveling on her own would be a big challenge for her. Even so, she wanted to give her young daughter all the support she needed to be successful in her budding career. Angela seemed to be blossoming, working for this particular organization. Her rather matter of fact attitude towards her long-time boyfriend was unusual, however. Pamela knew better than to pressure her. "Make sure you let us know where you're going—and when."

"I will," agreed Angie. "Hey, Mom, what about that guy who murdered his wife?"

"What?"

"That James Grant? You know. That politician. Didn't you guys hear about it on the news?"

"Oh, yes, dear, we heard about it," said Pamela. She had no intention of revealing to her impressionable daughter her potential involvement with the James Grant case.

"Maybe you can solve that murder, Mom," said Angie, "just like you solved those other ones."

"I don't think so, Angie," replied Pamela. "The police already have their suspect. They don't need my help on this one, evidently."

"Mom," said Angela, "I can't believe you'd let that stand in your way."

Like mother, like daughter, thought Pamela.

Chapter Eight

Again, Pamela found herself out of doors on a beautiful August morning surrounded by rolling grassy knolls, well-manicured flower beds, and stately old elm and maple trees that lined winding paths. A lovely place to be in any other circumstance than the one in which she found herself today. In a small isolated nook of the Heavenly Hills Cemetery, Pamela stood stoically along with Rocky, Joan, Willard, and several other faculty members from her department, as a minister dressed in a long white robe and golden chasuble intoned Bible verses over the coffin of Stacy Grant. An older couple—apparently the dead woman's parents–stood at the foot of the coffin, the woman sobbing uncontrollably. A large canopy on four tall posts covered the coffin, the grave, and the primary participants.

Pamela looked around at the large crowd. Everyone who was anyone in city government was in attendance. Political supporters from both the Grant and the Brewster camps dotted the hillside, looking down on the minister and the coffin. At a distance, camera crews lay in wait like jackals outside a recent lion kill. Beyond that, hidden among trees and prowling in the even more distant parking lot, local police officers watched for possible suspicious behavior. Everyone was there including the deceased's husband. He stood slightly apart from the other mourners between two guards, wearing the same clothes she had seen him in at the rally—now disheveled. His blank face was focused on the coffin with an unmoving rigidity. Pamela could not help but notice that he looked like a totally different person from the upbeat, confident politician she had met a few days prior.

"Blessed be the meek," spoke the preacher, followed by more words that Pamela couldn't hear. The religious leader held his arms above the coffin for a brief moment and then suddenly lowered his head and folded his hands. The assembled crowd followed his lead—except, of course, for the media and the police who maintained their watchful stances. Pamela kept her head down politely, but peeked to the side in an attempt to observe the responses of some of the key players in this morning's little drama. The Brewster entourage, she realized, was here primarily for show. They had no real concern for Stacy Grant or her family. If anything, they would probably try to waylay a reporter or two in order to solidify their demands that James Grant's name be removed from the ballot before November. Or, at least, that Grant be arraigned for his wife's murder as soon as possible. This last would, no doubt, lead to the former.

As the minister finished the graveside service, the parents of the deceased moved over to speak to the minister who closed ranks around them. This appeared to be the sign for onlookers to depart. Apparently, the coffin would not be actually buried until later. Some people turned immediately and began to walk up the grassy hill towards the parking lot. Others milled around chatting softly. Several proceeded downhill towards the minister and the coffin where they stopped to pay their respects to the deceased woman's parents.

"I'm going to speak to Stacy's parents," said Martin Dobbs, standing to the right of Willard and Joan.

"I'll go with you, Martin," added Willard. The two men headed off down the hill.

"What do you say, Pamela?" asked Joan, standing to her right. "Should we express our condolences?"

"I don't know the woman's parents," said Pamela. "And I don't—didn't—know *her* at all."

"All right," said Joan, "I'm going though." She looked at Pamela.

"You can go," said Rocky. "I'll wait here for you."

"No," said Pamela to Joan. "You go ahead Joan. You had actually met the woman." Joan hiked her purse up over her shoulder and headed as cautiously down the grassy slope as her two inch heels would allow.

"I don't mind waiting for you, Babe," said Rocky.

"It's all right, Rocky," said Pamela. "There's no reason to inundate that poor couple with a lot of strangers. I'm afraid people will do so just because this is a media circus." She gestured around at the cameramen, noticeable at the ridge of the hill. "They don't need an extra person intruding on their grief."

"It does look as if every TV station in town has sent a team, doesn't it?" asked Rocky.

"And then some," she agreed. "And add to the mix, all the local politicians."

"Which ones are they?" he asked.

"Over there to your left, in that group down by the edge of the canopy," she pointed discreetly. "The bald guy's the mayor—Hap Brewster."

"Oh, yeah," said Rocky. "I recognize him."

"And the guy next to him—the fat one with the long pointy nose and the suit much too dark for August—that's Victor Baines, his campaign director."

"Creepy," noted Rocky. "And the younger guy? The nerdy one on the other side?"

"That's his Communications Director," she replied. "I think Joan said his name is Kevin Sturges."

"The three of them look like a hit squad." Rocky ambled closer down the hill to get a better look at the mayor and his cronies. Pamela followed along.

"You may be speaking figuratively, Rocky," said Pamela, "but you may be more right than you know."

"Hit squad?"

"Yes," she said. "From what I've been hearing from Jane Marie, the Brewster gang pretty much controls local businesses. That is, no one opens or keeps a business in Reardon without Brewster's approval."

"Really?"

"And she would know. She's lived here all her life. Her husband works in the oil fields and he gets a lot of information from people in that industry. She's just sick about James. She was hoping he'd get elected and oust Brewster."

"A lot of residents of Reardon were, I guess," answered Rocky. "It's never been something that's concerned me—us—particularly."

"I know," she agreed. "He doesn't really have much to do with the university. Just the local businesses. And he's been mayor for as long as Jane Marie can remember. How many terms would that be?"

"Don't know. I've heard of some mayors in some small towns holding office for life."

"It certainly looks like that's what Brewster intends," she whispered, as they wandered far enough down the hillside to overhear the conversation taking place between Brewster and his two political lieutenants. Rocky turned towards his wife, his back towards the threesome and Pamela gazed adoringly into her spouse's face. The couple appeared as oblivious of the Brewster trio as any of the other funeral attendees who were standing around chatting idly.

"Make sure you get one of those reporters to interview the grieving parents," ordered Brewster to his Communications Director, Sturges. "The wife is still blubbering."

"She'll be very sympathetic," added Campaign Manager Victor Baines. "Distraught mother. If she blames the son-in-law on camera—even better."

"Don't worry," said Sturges. "I'll make sure they get good footage. Stuff that'll look bad for Grant."

"If this doesn't get him to officially drop out," said Brewster, "nothing will. I don't want to wait around for some damn trial. I want him out now!"

"Hap," said Baines, with a firm hand on the mayor's arm, "calm down! We've got the guy where we want him. Tried and convicted or just arrested and in jail, he's not going to be moving up any more in any polls."

"Yeah," smirked Brewster. "Well, see to it that he doesn't." The three men closed ranks and became even more agitated in their discussion—yet much quieter. Rocky and Pamela were unable to overhear anything else. They sauntered up the hill and towards the parking lot. As they passed one particularly leafy old tree, a man dressed incongruously in a grey raincoat and a rain hat—much too warm for this August day, appeared from behind the trunk.

"Dr. Barnes," he greeted Pamela. "Mr. Barnes." The tall, gangly man positioned himself in front of the couple, impeding their ascent.

"Detective Shoop!" cried out Pamela. "I'm surprised to . . . well, actually, I'm not surprised to see you here. Apparently, the entire Reardon police force is here for this funeral. I should have guessed that you'd be around somewhere."

"Detective," said Rocky, shaking hands with the officer. "Here looking out for my wife?" Pamela nudged him and sneered.

"So, Detective," said Pamela, "Does this massive outpouring of Reardon's finest indicate that our police officials may have some second thoughts about the guilt of James Grant?"

"I might ask you the same thing, Dr. Barnes," said the lanky detective, with a small nod at his sometimes civilian partner. "Did you know Stacy Grant, or are you and your husband merely looky-loo's?"

"I'm just an escort, Shoop," said Rocky with a shrug. "Just along for the ride, so to speak."

"Actually," explained Pamela, looking up at the tall man and being forced to squint in the bright sunlight, "I don't— didn't know her—or James, but some of my closest colleagues—Joan Bentley and Willard Swinton—did. Joan worked on James's campaign and Willard is quite close with James's campaign manager Martin Dobbs."

"Good answer," said Shoop, nodding slowly. "I'd hate to think that the two of you were doing any snooping out here."

"Snooping?" exclaimed Rocky. "No, sir. Not us. Just paying our respects. Enjoying the lovely weather, the beautiful scenery."

"Because if you were snooping, Dr. Barnes," continued Shoop, leaning in closely to Pamela's face, "it might make me very curious. It's just that I know that whenever you get mixed up in an investigation, Dr. Barnes, it's because you have suspicions and that when you have suspicions, things tend to go awry."

"Things don't . . . go awry, Detective," she countered, "because of my involvement. It's just that at times I've noticed when things were already . . . awry . . . at least, that's what I did in our past . . . adventures . . . and I merely pointed these . . . things . . . out to you. If you recall."

"I do recall, Dr. Barnes," said Shoop, with a nod, his eyes still focused on Pamela's face. "Now, here you are . . . at the funeral of the wife of a high profile murder suspect. It makes me wonder what you know—or at least—what you are thinking and what sort of trouble you may be planning on getting into."

"It seems to me, Detective," retorted Pamela, "that what you should be wondering is not what sort of trouble I might get into. If you genuinely believe that my presence is portentous, it seems to me you should be wondering just what my thinking might be with regards to the guilt or innocence of James Grant."

"Do you know something about Mr. Grant that impacts on his guilt in this case, Dr. Barnes?"

"No, Detective," she replied with a glimmer in her eyes— eyes that never wavered from Shoop's penetrating stare. "I don't *know* anything. But I do have my suspicions. And you know all about my suspicions, don't you, Detective?" She gave him a sudden smile, complete with fluttering eye lashes, grabbed Rocky's arm, and strolled past Shoop up the hill towards the parking lot.

"Home?" Rocky asked his wife.

"Yes," agreed Pamela. "I believe this has been a very productive funeral."

Chapter Nine

Pamela was so glad that the next day was Saturday and she was able to sleep in late. The past few days had left her feeling saturated with intrigue and conspiracy. At one point, she felt she was living in the middle of a Tom Clancy thriller. And she was just a bystander.

She pulled her flowered comforter up around her shoulders because the air conditioning in their house appeared to be running on all cylinders. She was freezing. Of course, not freezing enough to get up and change the thermostat. Just enough to wrap herself in as many covers as possible.

"Hey!" cried her husband, "you're taking all my covers!"

"I'm cold!" she retorted. Grumble, grumble, she heard, as Rocky rolled out of his side of the bed and lumbered out to the living room and lowered (or raised, she was never certain how to describe what one did to get a thermostat to work) the cooler. She drifted off and hadn't realized where he'd gone, when he arrived back with a tray of scones and coffee just the way she liked it—with lots of cream and no sugar. Rocky flipped on the television and joined her back in bed while they nibbled and sipped and watched the morning news.

First stop was local station WSTA which was airing a mini-documentary of the life and times of James Grant and his wife. How television stations managed to produce these lengthy, well-researched, thoroughly documented videos so quickly after a major event never ceased to amaze Pamela. It was as if the studio expected James Grant to kill his wife and they had his life story on film and ready to air. Of course, she reasoned, James was a public figure—and a popular one, given his challenge of Hap Brewster.   Even his wife had received a fair amount of press in her short, young life as an assistant district attorney.

"James Grant and Stacy Rollins met in college.   Both were from out of state and James's parents are now deceased. James is an only child." *Thank heaven for small favors,* thought Pamela.   It was agony enough for parents to experience the death of a child, but having a child arrested for murder somehow seemed worse.

The narrator continued, "While in college, both James and Stacy were exemplary students.   Both received academic scholarships throughout their undergraduate years.   James was the recipient of the prestigious Cleveland Scholarship which funded his entire three years of law school.   Stacy, likewise, won the Marymount Law Prize for Women which paid for her entire legal education.   Both graduated in the top five percent of their classes."

"The couple married in 2008, several years after their graduation from Grace University's College of Law," intoned the voice-over announcer as the screen showed stock footage of graduation portraits and wedding photos.   "Both were 28. James immediately opened his own firm with his long-time college friend Martin Dobbs.   Stacy Grant went to work for the local District Attorney's office, rising rapidly to become an Assistant District Attorney just last year.   The couple had no children."

WSTA's filmed history of the life and times of James and Stacy Grant concluded with the announcer's statement that James was being held in the Reardon city jail pending his arraignment.   Police officials offered no speculation concerning Grant's possible motive for his wife's murder. When the background film on James and Stacy Grant concluded and a regularly scheduled Saturday morning cartoon program came on, Rocky roamed the channels searching for additional information about the recent murder.

WRER was airing an interview that Ginger Cooper had conducted the previous day with Hap Brewster—no doubt the one he had persuaded her into doing when he caught her taping with James Grant in the park, Pamela thought. Rocky and Pamela watched the taped interview with special interest—comparing the presentation of the city's long-time experienced mayor, Brewster, with the footage on the young upstart who was vying for his job—and who might very well have snatched it–had it not been for his recent arrest. In this footage, Brewster was making his typical complaints about his opponent, so obviously the interview had been taped before the murder. It seemed incongruous for Brewster to be discussing Grant as if he were still merely a candidate—and not a murder suspect. The camera cut back to the female anchor in the studio.

"In our studio today, we have Mayor Brewster's Communications Director Kevin Sturges." The camera panned over to show the young man who had accompanied Brewster in the park. "Kevin, the mayor's main opponent is now sitting in jail accused of murder. How does this impact the mayor's campaign?" The camera panned further back to show the anchor and Sturges in profile, sitting across from each other.

"How do you think it impacts it, you ninny?" cried Rocky. "It makes Brewster a shoo-in!"

"Shh, Rocky," whispered Pamela. "I want to hear what this guy says." She scooted up against her headboard and pulled her comforter tight around her chin.

"Of course, Mayor Brewster is shocked and horrified to learn of the arrest of Mr. Grant," began the neatly dressed political operative, today wearing a navy blazer atop his typical yuppie outfit of chinos and blue shirt. "We would certainly prefer to win the election the old-fashioned way–by gathering the majority of the votes–not by default."

"But it does appear that Mayor Brewster will win the race come November, doesn't it?" suggested the anchor. "I mean, assuming no other candidate decides to run."

"I believe it's too late to file," said Sturges, with a shrug. "Of course, there are several other candidates running."

"But none making as strong a showing in the polls as James Grant was making, right?" She looked directly at the man seated across from her.

"No," agreed Sturges, "but you never know in politics." He laughed and smiled flirtatiously at the attractive anchor.

"It was actually fortuitous for the mayor that Grant was arrested when he was," continued the dark-haired woman, crossing one shapely leg over the other.

"I don't know what do you mean by 'fortuitous'—" said Sturges with a wide-eyed expression.

"Of course you know what she means, you son of a bitch!" sneered Rocky.

"Only that Grant seemed to be pulling ahead in the polls when he was arrested," explained the anchorwoman, slowly tapping her foot up and down provocatively.

"Yes," agreed the interviewee with a chuckle as he ran his hand through his hair, "but polls change."

"So they do," she agreed. The repartee between the two was becoming sexual, it seemed to Pamela. Or maybe she was imagining it. The young female anchor was exceedingly attractive and she obviously knew how to use her feminine wiles to charm a subject into responding. The interview continued for a few more minutes during which time Pamela and Rocky had an opportunity to finish their breakfast.

"Is there anything else on the other stations?" Pamela asked her husband and controller of the remote. Rocky pushed buttons, jumping from one local station to another. Reardon only had three local, network-affiliated stations and one public access station. The arrest of mayoral candidate James Grant was the hot topic on all of these. However, it didn't garner as much as a mention on the stations in the larger towns miles away.

"I guess a hotly contested political campaign—all tied into a murder—doesn't rate much more than a mention outside of our little community," she noted, licking crumbs from her fingertips. Candide made his morning appearance from underneath their bed and leaped up onto the covers demanding the crumbs.

"Yeah," agreed Rocky. "It's odd that the police haven't even speculated on Grant's motive. I mean, did you hear any of those reporters interviewing neighbors? I didn't. You'd think they'd find somebody who'd claim to have heard that couple fighting or that had seen something odd."

"Like what?"

"You know," he suggested, "when a couple is having marital troubles, it frequently—I'd say often—gets loud! The Grants have neighbors. Surely they must have heard something or suspected something if this James and his wife were fighting so much that it ultimately led to the guy whacking her."

"You'd think, wouldn't you?" she mused, giving Candide a snuggle but no treat. The dog gave a deep sigh as Pamela finished her coffee. "And," she added, "I met the man, and even though I only said a few words to him, he just didn't seem like the violent type. I mean, I pegged him for the type who would be very civil if he had an insurmountable misunderstanding with his wife."

"I guess anybody can become violent if given the right motivation," said Rocky, slurping from his cup. Candide attempted to cozy up to his master, but Rocky scooted him off the bed and the furry creature gave up his efforts and returned to his lazy, under-the-bed nap.

"What could the right motivation possibly be in this case, Rocky?" she asked, turning to her husband. "I met this man less than an hour before he supposedly committed this horrible crime—and I didn't see any sign that he was capable of or about to commit murder."

"Now, Babe," cautioned Rocky. "I hear the wheels turning in that devious little brain of yours. Don't start getting ideas. You heard what Shoop said. Stay out of this."

"Of course, I'm going to stay out of it, Rocky," she assured him with a hug. "Even if I wanted to get involved, it's not as if there's anything I can do. I mean, there's no sound clue. The police have their suspect. They don't need me to determine a suspect from the sound of some unknown voice."

"I don't know," he said, uncertainly. "I'm not sure that's enough to prevent you from snooping around if you're really determined."

"I'm not going to do any snooping," she said, kissing her husband on his cheek. "You can rest assured."

Chapter Ten

After a relatively quiet weekend, Pamela's Monday started out with a bang. She had barely arrived in her pleasant, home-like office and had barely put her lunch sack with one of Rocky's gourmet sandwiches inside in her mini-fridge, when Joan Bentley popped her head inside the door.

"I know you don't have class now!" began Joan, as she barged in, slamming Pamela's office door closed behind her. "We have to talk."

"I just got here," moaned Pamela as she slid into the cushions of her comfy couch and began to unscrew the top of her thermos. Joan sat primly, as usual, on the straight back chair beside the door.

"I just heard from Martin," Joan said.

"Martin?" asked Pamela, "You mean James Grant's partner?"

"And campaign manager," corrected Joan. Her upright posture was noticeably more severe than usual—indicative that Joan was on a mission.

"Yes," continued Pamela. "You're talking to him?"

"Actually," explained Joan with more animation than she usually exhibited, "Willard contacted me."

"You said Martin Dobbs contacted you," said Pamela, grimacing. Joan was on a roll and much further along in her journey than Pamela, who still maintained a blissful Monday morning fog.

"Martin contacted Willard and Willard called me."

"Willard's not here?" asked Pamela. It was not like Willard to make phone calls to them. If he needed to discuss something, he would typically wait until he saw Pamela at work. After all, his office was next door and all he had to do was tap on the adjoining wall.

"He called me from the jail," continued Joan, becoming even more expressive.

"Willard is at the jail?"

"Yes!" exclaimed Joan, now apparently getting to the meat of her message. "Martin has been the only person to actually visit James in jail, except, of course, the police. He is his attorney—and of course his best friend."

"I had heard on TV," contributed Pamela, "that James Grant is an only child and that both of his parents are dead. I don't know if that's a blessing or a curse, given his situation."

"I know what you mean," agreed Joan, hands pushing through her neatly coifed silver hair. "The poor man could certainly use some family support right now. Thank God he has Martin."

"Yes," said Pamela. "I can see that. But why is Willard there?"

"Evidently, Martin asked him to visit James. Martin says that James has become so despondent that he can't get him to even become involved in his own defense. James says he didn't kill his wife, but he still says he's guilty. Martin can't get any more out of him. He's stymied. Martin and Willard are close—so he asked Willard to talk to James. He thought that maybe James might be able to communicate more rationally with someone he didn't know as well. And—the important part—he thought Willard might be able to pick up on something in James's voice that might help him figure out how to defend him."

"Even if he's guilty?" asked Pamela, sipping her warm orange blossom tea cautiously.

"Especially if he's guilty," agreed Joan. "But he's not! Of course, Martin simply doesn't believe that he's guilty, but he's totally at a loss to figure out what did happen, because James won't—or can't—contribute to his own defense because he's so depressed about his wife's death."

"So?" asked Pamela, with a certain mounting excitement. "Did Willard detect anything unusual in James's voice?"

"Willard believes that James is telling the truth about his innocence." Joan leaned back in the chair and looked pointedly at Pamela.

"Willard has done some work on vocal cues related to deception," noted Pamela. "Although, most of that research suggests that there are precious few specific features that are mutually exclusive for truth and deception."

"I know that," said Joan, leaning forward again. "But Willard assured Martin that he was almost one hundred percent certain that James was being truthful about not killing Stacy."

"Maybe James believes he didn't kill his wife, but he really did," said Pamela.

"How could that be?" said Joan.

"I don't know," said Pamela with a shrug. "Maybe he killed her in a rage then forgot about it because he was so traumatized."

"For God's sake, Pamela!" cried Joan. "How can a scientific researcher come up with such fanciful ideas?"

"It's those fanciful ideas that allowed me to solve not one, but three murders, in the last few years!"

"So, you're telling me you don't believe in Willard's evaluation of James Grant?"

"No," said Pamela, "I do believe Willard. He's always very cautious. He'd never make a pronouncement like that unless he was positive."

"Anyway," continued Joan, "why I came in here, is because Willard—and Martin—want you to come down to the jail and talk to James."

"What?" she exclaimed. "I don't know the man. I mean, I just met him that one time. I doubt that my talking to him would add any more to his lawyer's evaluation of his honesty than Willard's."

"I don't know about that," said Joan. "All I know is that both of them—Willard and Martin—asked specifically for you to come to the jail. Surely, you won't refuse? I mean, a man's life is in the balance. If you can contribute something—anything—don't you feel a bit obligated to assist?"

"Joan!" she cried. "I have class. I have papers to grade."

"Pamela," said Joan, "no one is asking you to spend the day in the city jail. Just go talk to the man for an hour or so."

"Why would he agree to talk to me anyway?" She stretched her legs out and leaned back in the sofa cushion with a sigh.

"If Martin asks him to, he will, says Willard," Joan explained. "He's so defeated; he's a shell of the James you—we—remember from the rally."

"And if I go talk to him," she offered, "what is it that I'm supposed to be looking for? I haven't done any deception research like Willard has. I don't know what you would expect me to listen for."

"Just listen," said Joan. "Just talk. Let him talk. You're insightful. What harm can it do for you just to talk to him?"

"None, I guess," she responded with a deep sigh as she sank farther down into her sofa. The rays of the sun that had shone so brilliantly through her blinds just moments before, in a striped pattern on her floor, now turned to a dismal gray—as gray as she felt. This was not what she wanted to do. Just because she had solved those other mysteries didn't mean that she was chomping at the bit to solve every crime that occurred in her city. And Rocky! Oh, my, she didn't even want to think how he'd react if—when—he heard that she'd gone to the city jail to interview a murder suspect!

"All right. I'll go visit with James Grant. When am I supposed to do this?" she asked her friend who now had a smug look on her face.

"No time like the present!" said Joan brightly.

Chapter Eleven

She managed to postpone Joan's insistent demand, and schedule her jailhouse meeting with James Grant for later in the afternoon. Ungraded quizzes and last-minute prepping for her morning lecture provided undeniable excuses. Now, hours later, she stood at her desk, packing her belongings into her purse, gathering her thermos and books on her desk. A glance at her watch told her it was nearing three o'clock and her interview with James Grant was scheduled for 3:30 p.m. She headed out, locking her door behind her. The hallway was quiet. Willard and Joan were probably in class.

As she was leaving for the day, she dropped by the main office to check her mail box. She was standing by her cubby hole, thumbing through the various pieces of mail, when the departmental chairman, Mitchell Marks, came through, ushering an elegantly-dressed, middle-aged woman wearing a silver, silk designer suit.

"Mitchell," said the attractive woman, "I will expect that chili cook-off of yours to be a smash success! Just like last year's!"

"With your donation, Katherine," replied their chair in his typical dour fashion, "it's sure to be."

With a tinkling laugh, the woman gave Mitchell two quick social kisses on either side of his face. Then smiling, she turned and exited from the main office. Mitchell turned to return to his private domain, located beyond Jane Marie's small alcove. He noticed Pamela, standing before the wall of faculty mailboxes.

"Pamela," he greeted her warmly. "Just departing?"

"Looks like you found a donor for the chili cook-off?" she asked.

"Oh, yes!" he replied. "Katherine Brewster. She's always been very generous to our department."

"Katherine Brewster?" asked Pamela, "The mayor's wife?"

"The very one," responded Mitchell, heading back towards his office. Pamela followed him, eyeing Jane Marie as she passed her desk. The pert secretary gave her a wide-eyed shrug.

"I had no idea that the mayor's wife was interested in Grace," said Pamela. Mitchell wandered into his office and behind his desk. He seemed totally nonplussed when Pamela followed him in, uninvited.

"I don't know how interested she is in any other department," mused Mitchell, casually lifting his feet up onto the edge of his massive desk, "but she's very interested in Psychology."

"Really?" asked Pamela, propping herself on the edge of one of Mitchell's massive leather chairs that faced his desk.

"Probably has something to do with the fact that she was a Psych major when she was a student," noted Mitchell, reaching for a pipe from his desk pipe holder along with a long wooden match in a small bronze box beside it. University policy forbade smoking anywhere on campus, but typically it was not enforced in faculty offices.

"She's been funding the cook-off for some time?" asked Pamela.

"Since we started it," he replied. "In fact, if it weren't for Katherine Brewster, we never would have had our first cook-off. She has probably single-handedly been responsible for the success of our department's amazing, public, fundraising efforts, I'd say. More so than anyone else."

Pamela knew that all departments on campus relied on fund-raising efforts to survive. Yes, tuition paid for faculty salaries and basic upkeep, but departments had to raise massive amounts of extra money if they wanted to do any sort of building improvements or make any special purchases.

"If truth be told," he said bending to her, in a whisper, "after Charlotte Clark, Katherine raised more money for the computer lab than anyone else. Not to mention, all the recent improvements to the animal lab that Bob and Arliss are so proud of." Charlotte had been the Psychology Department's most prominent researcher and fundraiser before her murder in one of the booths of the aforementioned computer lab several years ago—a murder that had begun Pamela's erstwhile, crime-fighting career.

"When you say 'Katherine,'" ventured Pamela carefully, "you mean that she acts on her own? Not as a representative of her husband?"

"Don't really know, Pamela," said Mitchell with a shrug. Pamela gazed at her boss. Although she didn't consider him a close friend and colleague as she did Joan, Arliss, and Willard, she did feel relatively comfortable discussing important issues with him or pleading for his assistance when she needed it. In fact, Mitchell Marks had proven invaluable to her in a number of her criminal investigations. Mitchell puffed on his pipe. Sitting in the late afternoon light in front of his window, he reminded her of a Southern gentleman from the Civil War—just lacking the Confederate uniform. His massive head of wavy blond hair—complete with receding hairline—made him look like a modern-day Ashley Wilkes. "For all I know, Hap Brewster might be behind the donations, but it's Katherine who always arrives like clockwork to deliver the check. And a large check it is too."

"So you've known her for some time?" asked Pamela, trying not to wave away the potent odor of the pipe smoke.

"As long as I've been here—or as long as we've been doing the cook-off," he scowled. "Can't quite remember. But, she's a trooper. Quite a lady!" He smiled and seemed to drift off in reverie.

"You've never met her husband?" queried Pamela.

"Nope," said Marks with a shrug. "But, over the years, I've gleaned a lot about him from Katherine. I guess being the wife of such a notorious person makes a woman feel a bit—overshadowed. That may be why she likes to keep her contributions separate from his. My understanding is that she's independently wealthy—from a very socially prominent family. She's always very proper. At times, I've gotten the feeling that she's . . . embarrassed by her husband's mafia-style tactics. But she's too much of a lady to discuss them—or him."

"That's interesting," said Pamela, nodding. "But, of course, Mitchell, you're not too much of a gentleman."

"To discuss Hap Brewster?" he chuckled.

"He has been in the news a lot lately," she observed. "I mean, with this recent murder—and Brewster's main opponent accused."

"I know that a lot of people in this town—particularly at Grace," said Mitchell Marks, holding his pipe as a pointer, "would like to see Brewster ousted, I guess, because he's been mayor almost as long as some people have been alive. But, Pamela, small towns are not the same as the federal government. Reardon is not the only community with a life-long mayor—and having a long-serving mayor is not always a kiss of death. Some communities thrive under the tutelage and wisdom of an experienced leader."

"And you think that's the case in Reardon?" she asked.

"I think it could be a lot worse than many people think," he said.

"You don't believe in all of the allegations of corruption?" she asked.

"Pamela," he said in his most professorial voice, "wherever there is bureaucracy there is corruption. You think there's no corruption here at Grace?"

"I hope there's not as much as in our city government," she replied.

Mitchell harrumphed and used his metal pick to move the tobacco around in the bowl of his pipe.

"You really have been radicalized by this Grant faction, haven't you?"

"Radicalized?" she exclaimed. "Is anyone who supports someone other than the present mayor a radical?"

"No," he responded, "but if they encourage support of another candidate by suggesting that Hap Brewster's administration is corrupt, then they're going too far . . . ."

"But, Mitchell," she cried, somewhat amused, "isn't that the whole idea of elections? I mean, why would anyone ever run against anyone unless they believed that their opponent was doing something wrong? Maybe not illegal, but certainly ineffective?"

Marks held up his hands, waving the pipe. "Sorry, sorry!" he said calmly. "Not trying to start any sort of argument here, Pamela. Besides, it's a moot point, what with Grant's arrest, now, isn't it?"

"Although, given the rampant charges of corruption in the Brewster administration," she argued, "it's not much of a jump to suggest that Brewster—or his people—are involved in Stacy Grant's murder."

"What?" cried Mitchell, slamming his feet on the ground. "Now I've heard everything! The man was arrested standing over the body!"

"Mitchell," whispered Pamela, bending over his desk, "you and I both know from experience that murder investigations often take very strange turns."

"And you expect this one to turn away from Grant and point towards Brewster?"

"I don't expect anything, Mitchell," she replied. "But I do intend to keep an open mind and not assume that a man is guilty of murder based totally on circumstantial evidence."

"Like being caught in the act?"

"After the act," she corrected. "And how can you be impartial, Mitchell, when you have been regularly taking money from Hap Brewster's wife?"

"Pamela, Katherine has been donating money to the department—not to me personally—for many years. I hardly think that means she's trying to buy my political support for her husband. And I can guarantee you that it does not bias me—for or against—the suspect in this recent crime."

Pamela rose and started to leave. Mitchell stood and followed her to the door.

"Pamela, I'm sorry if I upset you," he said sincerely, hand on her elbow.

"Oh, you haven't upset me, Mitchell. It's fine that Mrs. Brewster is helping to fund the cook-off. I just have to get going. I have a 3:30 appointment to interview James Grant at the city jail."

With that, she smiled at her boss and practically floated out of the office.

Chapter Twelve

She sped out of campus and towards the downtown area several blocks away, attempting not to go too fast—after all, her ultimate destination was city hall, location of the Reardon Police Department. It had been several years since she'd received a speeding ticket and she was determined never to get another. Her wild driving habits had been a major bone of contention between her and her husband, so she drove with extreme caution, but as fast as the posted limit would allow. Knuckles white as she gripped the steering wheel, she sat stiffly and watched for every chance to take a traffic shortcut.

When she finally arrived at the two-story, ochre-colored stone building near the center of town, she had five minutes to spare. She zipped into the large parking lot and around to the rear of the building where she parked and sprinted up the five flights of high concrete steps leading to the back entrance to the police department where Shoop's office, the traffic fines window (a place she knew well), and the entrance to the city jail were located.

A large sign announcing "Reardon City Jail" and an arrow pointing down (rather unnecessarily, she thought) was painted in glaring red over the stairwell. It was totally incongruous to the rest of the signage which was all unwaveringly dull grey. Hiking her purse strap over her shoulder, she took a deep breath and headed down the short flight of stairs and through the swinging, metal, double doors directly beneath the red arrow. Inside, she found herself in a small lobby facing a clerk sitting behind a metal desk. The clerk glanced up at her expectantly.

"I'm Pamela Barnes," she said to the man, politely, stepping closer to the desk. "I'm supposed to have an appointment with James Grant."

"Barnes?" asked the clerk, as he looked down at a clipboard. She nodded. "Put your belongings in this," he ordered in a bored voice, pointing to a rectangular metal basket on a small counter to the right of the desk. Pamela did as asked, depositing her purse somewhat unwillingly and her jacket into the basket. Then, the clerk rose and opened a door behind him and disappeared. Pamela remained standing—as there were no chairs in sight—wondering if or when the man would return. A sense of being spied upon gripped her although no cameras were visible. Suddenly, the clerk returned through the door behind the desk.

"Follow the guard," he said to Pamela, and motioned toward the same door where a large, uniformed female stood. She turned and started to walk back the way she came, totally oblivious as to whether Pamela was following her or not. Pamela glanced around to make certain the clerk was speaking to her, but she was the only person in sight. She walked through the door and chased after the guard, walking quickly down a long, windowless hallway. The guard didn't even bother to turn around to see if Pamela was behind her. Pamela ran a few steps to keep up. The guard led her down the long hallway, turning several times left and then right before stopping before a windowed door. She turned and waited for Pamela to catch up.

"I need to check you," she said blandly as she opened the door and motioned for Pamela to enter. Pamela stopped abruptly, suddenly petrified. The guard looked bored as she quickly ran her hands down Pamela's body from shoulder to ankle in about three seconds. "If you need help, press the buzzer on the counter," she added as she exited.

"What?" Pamela started to say to the guard, turning around, but the woman had already disappeared from view. Pamela moved further into the small room, about the size of a large closet. Inside, she saw a built-in counter in front of a

Plexiglas window. A wooden, straight back chair was in front of the counter. She moved over and sat. On the counter was a built-in microphone—positioned directly across from its twin on the other side of the glass barrier. She saw the buzzer the guard had mentioned. A small, typed sign noted, "In case of emergency, press buzzer." *Oh, my god*, she thought. *What have I gotten myself into? What emergency could arise here? Are they suggesting that visitors here are in some sort of danger?* She looked at the Plexiglas pane separating her side of the room from the other side where obviously the prisoner would sit. Was it possible for a prisoner to break this glass? Surely not. But why would a visitor need an emergency buzzer? *Oh, well*, she said to herself. *Calm down. It's unlikely that James Grant is going to attempt to break through this panel and attack you, Pamela.*

A clanging noise banged in the distance, and suddenly a door in the room on the other side of the Plexiglas opened and another uniformed guard emerged, followed by James Grant wearing orange prison garb. The guard motioned to the chair in front of the counter with his stick, and James Grant moved into the seat without a word. The guard then turned and exited through the door he had entered, followed by the distinct sound of a massive metal door locking.

A strange stillness filled the tiny room. James Grant sat motionless on the opposite side of the pane; head bent, seemingly oblivious to Pamela's presence.

"Mr. Grant," she spoke into the microphone, uncertain that the device was even turned on. She couldn't hear any noise of Grant's movements through the Plexiglas window. She tried again. "Mr. Grant. James. I'm Pamela Barnes. We met at your rally the other day in the park. Your partner Martin Dobbs asked me to come speak with you."

"Dr. Barnes," said the prisoner finally in a voice totally different from the enthusiastic one she remembered from their first meeting. "I'm sorry Martin dragged you into this."

She waited for him to elaborate, but he continued to sit motionless, head down, eyes devoid of expression.

"Mr. Grant," she began. "James, if I may." She figured that one of them was going to have to speak and it apparently wasn't going to be James Grant. "James, Martin asked me to come talk with you because he wants me to see if I can find anything unusual about the—uh—recent events from a different perspective."

"I know, Dr. Barnes," said Grant, finally looking up at her with what she thought was probably the most forlorn expression she'd ever seen on a person's face. "I know that you have participated in several investigations. I'm sure you are quite good at what you do. Please don't be offended, but I think Martin is just grasping at straws."

"Did you kill your wife, James?" she asked abruptly.

"No," he replied immediately, but sadly. "But what difference does it make? She's gone."

"It makes a huge difference," she replied. "I'm speaking as a wife. I'm thinking how it would be if I were killed and my husband were unfairly accused of my murder. I would never want that because I love my husband and it would be horrible to imagine him accused—or worse—convicted of my death."

"If your husband loves you—and I'm sure he does," said Grant with a sad wry smile, "he probably wouldn't care what happened to him if he lost you."

"Maybe not at first," she noted, "but eventually I believe he would begin to wonder what really did happen. He wouldn't want my killer to go free."

Grant did not reply. Pamela hoped that she was making some headway, although she was certain that Martin Dobbs had already appealed to James Grant's sense of justice—and what surely must be a strong desire to see his wife's true killer apprehended.

"James," she continued, "I only have a short time to visit with you. I'd really like to hear you tell me exactly what happened the day of your wife's death. I know it will be hard, but I promise you, I will do everything I can to help Martin find evidence to track down Stacy's killer."

"It's all my fault," he cried, suddenly, dropping his head into his hands on the counter and sobbing pitifully.

"You killed her?"

"No," he sobbed, "but it's my fault this happened."

"I don't see how, James," said Pamela with as much tenderness as she could.

"And I never got a chance to tell her how sorry I was," he squeaked out the last few words, through increasing sobs.

"What were you sorry for?"

"We fought," he cried, biting his lower lip in a useless attempt to hold back his tears. "We had a horrible fight the night before. We never fought, but I was spending so much time on the campaign and she just got fed up and one thing led to another—and she told me to get out."

"She kicked you out of the house?" asked Pamela, "You mean, she did this the night before–the rally?"

"Yeah," he moaned. "I told Martin this, but he thinks I shouldn't mention it because it makes me look bad—but, so what? I do look bad. I am bad. If we hadn't fought, this wouldn't have happened."

"I don't see how," said Pamela. "You didn't kill her, did you?"

"No!" he screamed. "I told you! I didn't kill her, but I wasn't there to protect her! I slept in my office the night before—it happened. The person who did this must have had the opportunity to get into our house or figured out Stacy was alone because I wasn't there! If I'd been there, I know she'd be alive today."

"You don't know that, James," argued Pamela. "If you didn't kill Stacy, someone else did. We don't know who that person is or why they did it—but it's quite possible that it has nothing whatsoever to do with the fact that you and Stacy had an argument and you spent the night in your office. Quite possibly, the killer would have done exactly the same thing if you'd spent the night in your own house and gone to work just like every other day. Remember, your wife was killed late in the afternoon while you were at the rally. This may have nothing to do with your fight. I mean, you aren't with your wife every minute of the day. Even if you'd been at home that night, you still would have gone to work and to the rally. Stacy still would have been at home that afternoon when the killer arrived."

"I don't know," he said, voice wavering. Maybe, Pamela thought, she could reason with him—or at least gather some pertinent information.

"What did you fight about?" she asked.

"The amount of time I was spending on the campaign," he replied. "Nothing new. We were fighting about it more and more, but that night it blew up."

"Had you ever spent the night in your office before?"

"No, that was the first time. It wasn't comfortable. I hated every minute of it and all I wanted to do was apologize and go home."

"Did anyone on your staff know you spent the night in your office?"

"I don't know—maybe. Even if they did, they wouldn't necessarily assume it was because Stacy and I were having marital troubles. I didn't really discuss things like that with anyone—even Martin—although I guess he figured out that Stacy was peeved with me about all the extra duties he was piling on."

"Take me through your movements from your fight with Stacy until the next day when you returned home and found her."

"Oh, god," he sighed, obviously not relishing remembering, let alone describing the events. "We had a pretty loud screaming battle that night. She ordered me out and I just left—didn't even pack a bag. It was lucky that I keep an extra shirt in my office and a razor or I would have been a mess at the rally the next day."

"So, after you fought, you went directly to your office. Was anyone there?"

"No, it was about eleven at night. The place was dark."

"What about the next morning?"

"I couldn't sleep. I felt just terrible. I kept debating whether I should call her and apologize, but I decided I'd wait and talk to her in person the next day after she got home from work. I wish now I'd called her earlier—maybe this wouldn't have happened . . . ."

"Not necessarily," said Pamela. "You don't know the reason Stacy was killed. If a murderer is determined, they won't stop until they accomplish their goal. It might not have done any good no matter what you did."

"But her last memory of me wouldn't be filled with hatred."

"James," said Pamela, attempting to reach through the glass window and only succeeding in touching his finger tips with hers. "I have a feeling her memories of you were all good ones. And here I'm speaking as a woman and a wife. You have to have faith in that thought. Your fight was because of circumstances caused by your campaign—not some innate personality defect of yours that she couldn't tolerate. I'm guessing that in time the two of you would have worked out your differences."

"Maybe," he replied.

"Hold that idea in your heart and concentrate on doing the most positive thing you can do now for your wife—find her killer."

"All right." He looked at her with the same sad face, but his gaze was now direct.

"When you woke up in your office the next morning, what happened then?"

"Not much. It was a regular day. Martin came in first. We did regular law office stuff—and a lot of campaign activities. Later in the afternoon, some volunteers arrived to help get ready for the rally. Then around four we all piled in our cars and headed for the rally."

"Did you notice anything unusual about the rally?"

"No, we'd done several before and this one seemed about the same. Of course, the media showed up—and Brewster and his crowd. But other than that, nothing seemed strange to me."

"Did you speak to or see Stacy at all during the day?"

"No, I was giving her time to cool down. I planned to see her after the rally when I went home. I knew she'd be there before me probably. She usually gets home around four. Oh, but she did call me right after the rally ended. That's what sent me home so fast."

"She called you?"

"Yes, I told the police. She called me at the rally and told me to come home right away and then she hung up. I don't know if that had anything to do with the call she made to 911—you know—whether it was before or after that."

"Did you actually talk to her?"

"Uh, yes."

"I mean, she didn't leave a message or anything."

"No," he said, thinking. "As soon as I saw our home number, I answered immediately. It was about the time that Ginger Cooper was starting to interview Brewster. I was just standing there listening to them."

"Try to remember exactly what she said."

"I think she said, 'Come home' or maybe 'Come home now' or something like that. I just jumped in my car and took off."

"Did you say anything to her?"

"I may have, but I think she hung up immediately—and that scared me. I mean, she didn't even wait for me to respond. So I figured whatever she needed me for at home was serious . . ."

"Do you remember the time of Stacy's call?"

"No, I'm sorry. Just that it was after my interview at the rally—during the Brewster interview."

"You don't by any chance know what question Brewster was answering when Stacy called?"

"You think that's important?"

"I'm just trying to develop a time line. It may—or may not—be important."

"I think he was just getting started. I don't remember if she'd even asked him a question yet." Grant scowled. Pamela perceived it a good sign that James was able to focus—if only for a moment—on his political opponent's platform.

"Okay, anyway. You drove home as fast as you could. Now, tell me exactly what happened when you got there."

"Dr. Barnes, I've gone over this part again and again for the police. I pulled up out front and I could see that the front door of our house was wide open. That scared me right away. I ran into the house calling for Stacy. She was lying on the floor of the kitchen. She was bleeding—from a huge gash in the back of her head. Oh, my God! If I'd just been there minutes before. It must have just happened. I bent down and tried to find a pulse. I couldn't. I tried to give her mouth to mouth. I tried but nothing—nothing helped." Repeating the story again had drained the young politician.

"Did you see or hear anyone else in your house?"

"No, but I wasn't looking for anyone. I was only concerned with Stacy."

"About how long after you discovered your wife on the floor was it before the police arrived?"

"Almost immediately. I had barely started to do the mouth-to-mouth and some uniformed guy grabbed me and handcuffed me. Another one read me my rights. At that point, I realized Stacy was gone—and nothing else really mattered."

"What about the candlestick? That they say is the murder weapon?"

"I guess I remember seeing it lying on the floor next to Stacy. It was one of a set that we had on our fireplace mantel. Stacy's parents gave those to us for our wedding. I may have moved it or picked it up at some point, but truly I don't remember. All I remember is seeing Stacy and trying to help her."

"James, can you think of anyone who might want your wife dead?"

"No, no one."

"Your wife worked for the DA's office. Has she prosecuted anyone who might have come back for revenge?"

"Stacy never mentioned anyone that she sent away that she ever thought would be some sort of risk to her. Of course, there might have been and she didn't tell me—or she didn't know herself."

"What about you? Is there anyone who might want to hurt you by killing your wife?"

"I can't imagine anyone."

"Not even Hap Brewster?" she suggested, with a raised eyebrow.

"What?" he asked, apparently genuinely flabbergasted. "You don't kill people who disagree with you over politics."

"Oh, really?" she noted. "You think Hap Brewster is totally above such a thing?"

"Dr. Barnes," he said with a shake of his head, "I have no love for Brewster or his crowd, but they're not murderers."

"Let's hope you're right," said Pamela with a shrug. "But someone is a murderer, James. And if it's not you, then who?"

Chapter Thirteen

As she climbed the short flight of stairs leading from the Reardon city jail to the City Hall parking lot, she ran smack dab into her friend and nemesis Detective Shoop, ostensibly on his way back to his office from the parking lot.

"Dr. Barnes," he exclaimed in his typical deadpan manner, "as I live and breathe." He had stopped in his tracks and was now barring her way, leaving her stranded on the next-to-the last step from the basement jailhouse. The result was that the tall, gangly policeman hovered over her even more like some predatory gargoyle—his open raincoat flapping like wings as he gestured his greeting to her. "What brings you to City Hall? Surely, you're not interfering—I mean—messing around in a police case, are you? It wouldn't by any chance be the James Grant murder investigation, would it?"

"Detective," she replied, ducking under his outstretched arm and leaning against the banister where she recovered her equilibrium. "How delightful to see you again. You must be on your way back to your office. Please don't let me detain you." She scooted around him, aiming for the outside, double-glass door entrance to the building.

"Oh, Doctor," cried Shoop, grabbing her by the elbow. "Please do come up to my office for a chat." He gave her arm a decided squeeze and immediately bounded up the flight of stairs leading to the Police Department on the second floor. Pamela sighed and followed him. Surely, this would be a brief social visit and she could be quickly on her way.

Shoop's office was just inside the back door entrance to the second floor and immediately to the right. His, like most of the detectives' offices in the Reardon Police Department, was small and encased with wood paneling up to waist height with glass partitions the rest of the way up. She always thought how awful it would be to have such an office because it would allow the resident no privacy whatsoever. Inside the office, she recognized Shoop's cluttered desk and his torn and tattered, small, plastic sofa. One tiny window overlooked the parking lot. In the corner, Shoop's space heater stood vigil. Thankfully, it wasn't running on this sweltering August day, but Shoop seemed to have a persistent cold and every time she'd been in this office in the past, the space heater had been churning out warmth—often too much.

"Sit, Dr. Barnes," Shoop ordered, as he flung his dilapidated raincoat over the top of a wooden coat stand, moving behind his old-fashioned desk. She positioned herself primly on the edge of the sofa, knowing full well that probably a month's worth of junk food had slid into the cracks and crevices. "I'm guessing that you were down in our jail visiting Mr. Grant. Am I right?"

"He is allowed visitors," she retorted. After working together—sometimes cooperatively and sometimes not—Shoop and Pamela had developed a grudging respect for each other. Nevertheless, he needled her whenever they worked together and she tried to give as good as she got. Theirs was a relationship filled with rivalry.

"So, it was a social call?" he asked, leaning back in his squeaky roll-chair. "I didn't realize that the two of you were friends. I mean, you certainly didn't indicate such when I saw you at his wife's funeral the other day." He leaned over his desk and leered at her.

"If you must know, I was asked to talk to him—by his lawyer," she replied with a huff.

"And why would that be?" he asked, tapping a pencil on his desktop.

"I don't have to answer that, Shoop," she shot back. "I'm not on trial. You don't have any authority to question me."

"If you attempt to meddle in our investigation, Dr. Barnes. . . ."

"What investigation?" she cried. "My understanding is that there is no investigation. You—and your colleagues–are convinced that you have Stacy Grant's killer, so all further investigation—if there ever was any investigation to begin with—is over."

"The state of our investigation is not something I'm at liberty to share with you," he replied, gnawing on the end of his pencil.

"Unless, of course," she suggested, airily, "some sort of sound clue turns up and you need my expertise."

"We're not expecting any such thing," he noted somberly.

Pamela was quickly getting annoyed and tired of this banter. She glanced at her watch and saw that it was much later than she'd thought.

"Detective," she said politely, "I really must be going . . . ."

"Dr. Barnes," replied the tall man in a much softer voice, his eyes piercing into her, "I really would like to know just what you're doing involved in this case. I can get a subpoena if I have to, but given as how you and I have worked together on a number of investigations—successfully worked together, I might add—I would appreciate whatever insight or information you think you have in regards to this case."

"Why?" she demanded. "If I suggest an avenue for you to investigate, will you follow it just because it's me asking?"

"I can't promise . . . ."

"I didn't think so," she answered, standing and preparing to leave.

"Dr. Barnes," he said, "truthfully, I'm not personally even involved in the Grant investigation—so anything you tell me would be just conjecture. But, I do promise you, that I have nothing but respect for your instincts—I would be foolish not to respect them—and if you are looking into anything at all connected to this murder, I will not treat your concerns lightly."

"I'm stunned, Shoop," she replied, trying to suppress a smile, "at your honesty. And I, too, have great respect for your capabilities. I believe we have made a good team in the past. At the moment, all I can say is that I have James Grant's version of what happened—which is probably pretty much the same as what your investigators have. I need to think about what he told me and determine if I see any discrepancies."

"And do you? See any discrepancies?"

"As I said, I need to think about it. Maybe."

"Hmm," replied Shoop, continuing to chew his pencil end. "When you start to see discrepancies, Dr. Barnes, I keep my eyes open."

"You do that, Detective," she said and, with that, she opened the door and exited Shoop's office and headed out the back entrance of City Hall. Shoop stood and walked behind her to the door, following her out of the department with his eyes.

Chapter Fourteen

When she finally arrived home, she was exhausted. It had been an excruciatingly long day—and the most intense parts had come at the end. The jailhouse visit with the sad, accused murderer James Grant and the unexpected stop at Shoop's office had drained her. Now, she found herself wrapped in her comfy terrycloth robe, slumped in her bedroom easy chair, legs up on her hassock grading a set of quizzes she had given in her morning lecture class. Candide cuddled against her slippers on the hassock. She could hear Rocky futzing around in the kitchen. As usual, he had prepared them a delightful dinner—tonight's offering was a chicken salad with grapes, celery, and walnuts—light but tasty in one of Rocky's special dressings. She assumed he was now busy cleaning up. She should probably be doing that chore, but her dear husband was able to discern immediately on her arrival that she'd had a miserable day and he sent her off after supper to relax—if you could consider grading papers relaxing.

She took a deep breath and a pause from her grading as she glanced at her watch. It was almost time for the local evening news and she was anxious to see what—if anything— would be reported about James Grant's murder case. Grabbing the remote from the end table next to her chair, she flipped the "on" button and turned to channel six—WRER. Ginger Cooper was anchoring the news tonight and she led with the top story—Stacy Grant's murder.

"Reardon's District Attorney's office today announced that DA Charles Findlay will personally prosecute the case against accused murderer James Grant. Findlay said he felt a special obligation to undertake the task himself because the victim, Stacy Grant, had been an assistant DA in the Reardon bureau."

The screen switched to a video of an attractive older man, with a full head of snowy white hair, speaking in front of a hive of microphone-toting reporters in front of the City Hall that Pamela knew so well.

"Stacy was a co-worker and a friend," said Findlay, his rich mellow voice resonating. "The DA's office will not rest until we bring her killer to justice."

The screen returned to Ginger Cooper in the studio, focusing on the face of the pretty green-eyed redhead.

"In related news," she said, "the coroner has announced the autopsy results for Stacy Grant. Cause of death is said to be blunt trauma to the head. No secondary causes were determined.

"Oh, my," sighed Pamela, setting down her stack of quizzes and stretching her legs. The movement caused the little dog lying on top of her feet to whine in annoyance. "None of this looks good for James," she said out loud.

"What doesn't look good for James?" asked her husband, wandering into their bedroom and plopping down on the edge of their bed.

"Just the autopsy report," she replied. "Blunt trauma to the head."

"Did you expect something else?" he asked, wiping his hands with a dish towel.

"I guess I hoped maybe they'd find something in her system or something."

"How would that help?" he asked, leaning back.

"I don't know. I'm just gathering information."

"Something you do so well," he assured her. He stood up and headed back to the kitchen. "Are you ready for dessert?"

"Dessert?" she asked. "How am I ever going to get rid of these thighs?"

"I love these thighs," he replied, walking over to her chair and squeezing an exposed area of flesh.

"You won't if I keep eating your desserts," she pouted. "What is it?"

"A blueberry cobbler."

"Just a few spoonfuls," she said sheepishly.

"Okay," he agreed and headed off.

"I'll just feed most of it to you, Candide," she said to her pet who, upon hearing his name, perked up and rushed up to her and began licking her face.

"Hey, now! Don't get carried away!" she said to Candide, pushing him away from her cheek. Rocky returned with a small bowl of crispy covered purple fruit, topped with a dollop of whipped cream. "Rocky! This looks fattening!"

"We'll share," he offered, sitting on the edge of the hassock and dipping the spoon into the dessert. He then aimed the spoon into her mouth and she nibbled off a small amount. Candide attempted to intercept the spoon on its way to its target but was unsuccessful, so he leaped off the hassock and pranced out to the kitchen to eat his regular dog food. Rocky finished what blueberry cobbler Pamela had left on the spoon.

"Yum," she moaned. "Why do you do this?"

"Make dessert?"

"Why do you torture me like this? You know I'm trying to lose weight and you go and make these incredibly delicious things. How can I resist?"

"You can't resist my desserts—or me," he said with a sexy smile.

"You aren't fattening. Your desserts are." She gave him a a look of annoyance. He continued to nibble the cobbler and offered her a bite from time to time. She consumed what she was offered without additional complaining.

"Anything on the news about your friend James Grant?" he asked, wiping the spoon clean slowly with his lips, a movement that did not go unnoticed by his wife.

"The DA—Findlay–is going to prosecute the case himself."

"With Findlay prosecuting the case, it might speed things up."

"I'd think it would slow things down. He's probably pretty busy. Who knows when he'll have time to schedule himself for trial?"

"You'd think he'd want to get right to it. He's probably pretty upset that someone killed one of his assistants."

"I don't know. Maybe. I don't know how any of this will affect James. I know Martin has an investigator working for him. I don't know what he's looking for, but I'm guessing he'll need time to produce information that will help James."

"And, of course," added Rocky, giving Pamela one of his knowing looks, "you'll need time to figure out who really killed the woman."

"For heaven's sake, Rocky!" she cried. "Why does anyone think that just because I helped with some police investigations before, that I'm going to be able to produce evidence that will exonerate James?"

"Whatever you do, Babe," he said somberly, "please keep a low profile. You know what happened before. You get going and then you get headstrong and then you get in trouble."

"I promise I'll be very discreet," she said with a raised hand.

"Did you learn anything today when you visited the guy in prison?" he asked.

"The city jail," she corrected, "and his name is James. He's actually a nice guy—and heartsick over the death of his wife. He blames himself for it. Not because he did it, but because he wasn't there to prevent it."

"I can understand that," said Rocky, rubbing his wife's bare legs. She had a feeling that he had another type of dessert in mind now that he'd finished off the blueberry cobbler.

They had been ignoring the news broadcast, playing softly in the background. As Rocky was starting to nuzzle her ear, Pamela glanced up at the television set.

"Look at that!" she exclaimed. Rocky somewhat grudgingly leaned back on the hassock and glanced over to the

TV. A slick commercial, complete with catchy jingle and pulsing music was advertising the candidacy of Hap Brewster. An animated Brewster was presented looking like some type of Superman hero, slaying villains, including one that closely resembled James Grant. The commercial showed that particular villain being soundly flung into a jail cell by the super Brewster.

"Why does he need to advertise?" she asked her husband. "I mean, he doesn't have any viable competition now that James is in jail."

"Maybe he's afraid James won't be in jail for long," suggested Rocky.

"Just look at that, Rocky," she said, pointing at the screen. Rocky focused his attention on the clever political ad designed to capture the attention and votes of Reardon residents. "It's very good."

"You mean the ad is good," he said in clarification. "Not the content."

"No, I mean, yes," she replied, flustered. "It's a very sophisticated commercial. It totally glosses over Brewster's faults. It doesn't even mention James, but it hints at his problems. Very sneaky."

"I see what you mean," he nodded. "Far superior to your run-of-the mill, local, political ad. Most of those look like televised, wanted posters."

"I know. This one is well done. Too bad James doesn't have the same person doing his ads—maybe he could get some press that would help his case. He could use some good publicity."

"Surely his law partner could arrange for that," suggested Rocky, now totally having given up on getting any romance in the near future.

"I'm afraid that's the least of Martin Dobbs's concerns now. He's focused on exonerating James at best—and defending him in court at least."

"But it does seem like overkill, don't you think?" he asked. "I mean, why does Brewster need to exert himself in the campaign when his primary opponent is, for all intents and purposes, out of the race?"

"I guess he just wants to be sure," she replied. "Nail in the coffin mentality. Cross the t's and dot the i's."

"I wonder," mused Rocky. At that moment, Candide wandered back into the bedroom, evidently satiated from a nice meal of dog food. He looked from Pamela to Rocky with his soulful black eyes and then glanced at the bedroom door.

"He wants to go out," said Pamela with a sigh. "I should do it. After all, you cooked and cleaned up."

"Stay where you are," replied Rocky. "Finish those quizzes. Candide and I both need some fresh air. Don't we, fellow?" Candide responded to his name and to the fact that Rocky was rising and heading out of the bedroom. He began prancing at Rocky's feet with a happy bark. Man and dog disappeared into the other room. Pamela stared at the television and thought of the amazing commercial for Hap Brewster. It hadn't been created overnight, she realized. It was a professional production that probably took many weeks to do and yet it seemed somehow incredibly *apropos* to events of the last few days—what with the villain character being tossed into the mini-jail by the super Brewster character. It could all be coincidence, but she doubted it. She wondered what Martin Dobbs would think when he saw it.

Chapter Fifteen

It had been hard for her to concentrate on her morning classes. Now, as her second class was nearing its end and the students were working in groups completing a mini-project related to discernible language differences, Pamela found herself daydreaming about the intriguing case of Stacy Grant's murder while she wandered around the lecture hall on the second floor, next door to her office. The students were all totally engaged in the activity and all she seemed to need to do was indicate her presence and willingness to assist them. She checked her watch and noticed that only ten minutes of class time remained. She sauntered back down the aisle to the lectern at the front of the hall.

"Don't forget," she announced, "you need to turn in your group's responses before you leave." The students seemed to moan as a unit, but she noticed noises of paper and writing and an increased level of talk as they worked to complete the brief assignment.

One group finished and gathered their belongings and began to leave. One of the members walked up to Pamela and handed her a paper. Pamela quickly glanced down the responses to check to see if the group had followed directions. Assured that they had, she smiled at the student. A second group finished and then a third. Eventually all groups had completed the in-class project and had submitted it to Pamela before they left. As the last student departed, she double-checked to make certain that she had received a paper from each of her six groups.

"Dr. Barnes," said a female student, causing Pamela to look up into the face of a young woman who typically sat near the back of the lecture hall. "Excuse me for bothering you, but I'm wondering if I might ask you a question."

"Of course, uh, Mindy," she guessed at the student's name. She tried to memorize each of her students' names, and although she found it fairly easy to remember the names of the students who talked a lot in class or who visited her frequently, it was difficult at times to remember the names of students who tended to remain anonymous—as did this young woman. "What can I do for you?" She smiled warmly, encouraging this apparently, shy student to speak.

"Dr. Barnes, I was working on James Grant's campaign," replied the girl, looking down. "I met Dr. Bentley when we were stuffing envelopes one day. She said she was trying to get you to help with Mr. Grant's campaign."

"She succeeded," said Pamela, with a laugh. "Dr. Bentley can be very persuasive."

"Yes," agreed Mindy. "One time she and I were sitting at a table in the campaign office working on folding flyers and she was telling me about you and how you had helped the police solve some murders in the past."

"She probably exaggerated my involvement, Mindy," said Pamela. "I've offered my expertise in acoustic technology to local officials in a few instances, but that's all. Nothing very grand."

"Not according to Dr. Bentley," Mindy argued. "And Dr. Barnes, I was thinking that maybe now that Mr. Grant is in jail, maybe it would be a very good time for you to help out again."

"Oh, Mindy," chuckled Pamela, flattered but intent on diffusing this student's and any student's conception of her as some sort of local crime-fighter, "I think you have a distorted view of what I've done for the police. Truly, my efforts in helping the police have been minimal—and, besides, my expertise is in acoustics—sound. There really isn't any need for my skills in Mr. Grant's case."

"I think you underestimate your ability, Dr. Barnes," said Mindy intently. "I listen to your lectures and I see how you think things through so carefully. Everything you say in class is all about how scientists need to use evidence to build hypotheses. I think your hypothesis should be that Mr. Grant did not kill his wife. Isn't that how a scientist would start? Then, you could search for evidence that would support that hypothesis, couldn't you?"

"Yes, Mindy," she replied. "That's exactly what a scientist would do. But just because a scientist hypothesizes something, doesn't mean that he—or she—will eventually be able to support that hypothesis. Sometimes hypotheses are not supported."

"But, Dr. Barnes," Mindy pleaded, "I'm just sure that Mr. Grant didn't kill his wife! He couldn't! He's so nice!"

"Just how is it that you got involved in Mr. Grant's campaign, Mindy?" Pamela asked.

"My family has lived here as long as I can remember, Dr. Barnes," she said sadly, "and my parents run a small printing company downtown—Gregson Printing."

"Yes, I've heard of it," said Pamela.

"Hap Brewster has made my parents' lives intolerable," the girl continued. "When James Grant announced that he was running against Brewster, my parents were elated. They thought that maybe some of the abuse and intimidation they had experienced from the Brewster crowd over the years would stop. They were devastated when Mr. Grant was arrested. I told them I know he didn't kill his wife, but they say it doesn't matter because with him in jail—even if he gets out—it'll be too late to stop Hap Brewster."

"Not necessarily," said Pamela to the young woman, putting a hand on her shoulder. "I wouldn't give up, Mindy. James Grant has a number of excellent people on his team."

"You, Dr. Barnes?"

"I've been volunteering, but I think his greatest help is his partner Martin Dobbs."

"Oh, yes! Mr. Dobbs is amazing! He's always at the campaign headquarters—well, I say headquarters—but it's really just their office."

"Mindy, were you at the campaign headquarters the night before Mr. Grant was arrested?"

"Yes," she replied. "It was exciting. The poll had just come out showing Mr. Grant moving ahead of Brewster. Everyone was so excited. The rally was scheduled for the next day and we were all so busy getting posters and flyers ready."

"Was Mrs. Grant there?"

"I don't think she was that night. She did stop by once in a while. But not that night."

"Was Mr. Grant there that you remember?"

"I believe he was—at least at one point. He would stop and help out every so often—and, of course, it was his law office too, so sometimes he was there working on cases that weren't related to the campaign."

"How late did you stay that night?"

"I don't know, maybe midnight," she answered. "Is this important information, Dr. Barnes? Will it help you to support the hypothesis that Mr. Grant is innocent of his wife's murder?"

"I don't know, Mindy," she said, "but as a scientist, you know, we need all the information we can get—even if some of it eventually turns out to be unnecessary."

"Thank you, Dr. Barnes," sighed Mindy. "And thank you from my parents too."

"Don't thank me yet, Mindy," said Pamela. "I haven't done anything." She guided the young woman down the lecture hall's center aisle and out the doorway, bidding her farewell and then entering her office on the right.

Once inside, she grabbed her thermos of tea and got her sack lunch from her mini-fridge. Then she plopped down onto her couch and slid out of her high heels and set her nylon-covered feet up on the cushions. Two hours of lecturing always made her exhausted and famished. Rocky had outdone himself today, providing her with a sandwich of turkey, greens, and chipotle sauce on asiago cheese bread. He also included some fresh kiwi fruit sections. The tea of the day was persimmon—unique and tasty.

She was enjoying her midday meal and contemplating her heart-to-heart talk with her student Mindy when her two best friends and colleagues—Joan and Arliss—came sauntering into her office unannounced. Of course, Joan was the only one doing any sauntering; Arliss trudged most places now, being almost a full nine months pregnant and looking it.

"Oh, Pam," moaned Arliss, "can we trade places? I really need to put my feet up and if I sit on your desk chair, I'll probably slide off onto the floor."

"Of course, little mother," replied Pamela, rising and guiding her friend into the nicely warmed spot on the sofa. Arliss slid cautiously down and lifted her legs up onto the cushions with apparent agonizing difficulty. Pamela moved over to her desk chair and slid easily into place. On the way, she tossed her lunch sack into the waste basket.

"All she does is whine," noted Joan, as she sat unobtrusively on the straight wood chair by the door. "I don't remember all this drama when I had my two boys."

"Would you like something to eat, Arliss?" asked Pamela.

"No," said her curly-haired friend from her lounging position, "I'm starving, but my doctor has me on a strict diet. I thought I was supposed to be eating for two!"

"So, does your OB give you any estimation as to when we should expect this little Goodman?" asked Pamela as she sipped her remaining tea.

"Any day, he says," replied Arliss, her head barely visible over her tummy mound on the sofa, "and it can't be any too soon for me. I can barely breathe."

"I bet Bob will appreciate not hearing all the wa-wa too," added Joan flippantly. She fingered the gold buttons on her stylish navy jacket.

"Oh, Joan," scolded Pamela, "this is all new to her. Don't be so nasty."

"You'd think no one else ever had a baby," said Joan, glaring at Arliss.

"Stop!" Pamela scowled. "It's all right, Arliss. Just hang in there. But get as much sleep as you can now, because when the baby arrives, you won't be getting much at all."

"I know," Arliss replied. "I just want to be able to breathe and to see my feet." She moaned again and reached down to try to rub her feet without any success.

"They're still on your legs," chided Joan. Then she turned to Pamela at her desk and said, "Martin tells me you were able to visit James in the jail yesterday."

"Yes," Pamela replied.

"Oh, my!" exclaimed Arliss. "That must have been exciting, Pam! I've never been inside a jail before. What was it like?"

"I don't know what—if any—good it did. I do think he opened up to me. He's so despondent that he doesn't seem capable or interested in assisting in his own defense."

"That's what Martin said," noted Joan. She smoothed her white pleated skirt down.

"I think—at least—I hope I got through to him on that account. I tried to convince him that his wife would want him to find her killer. That he couldn't allow his wife's killer to roam free. I hope that argument struck home and got him to at least cooperate in Martin's investigation."

"That would certainly be an improvement," said Joan, "at least according to the way Martin described his reactions."

"I got him to go over his actions before he found Stacy," said Pamela, "in detail. He probably had explained this to the police, but I'm sure they were only interested in getting information that would confirm their belief in his guilt. I made him describe everything I could think of that might explain who killed Stacy—assuming that James didn't."

"That's what we're all assuming," insisted Joan. "Did he tell you anything that would help?"

"I'm not sure," she mused, elbows on her desk as she sipped her tea. "I'm still sorting out some of the things he said."

"Such as?" asked Arliss from her prone position on the sofa. Pamela could hear her voice but couldn't see her face behind her tummy.

"One thing, I'm afraid, may make him look guiltier if the police get a hold of it."

"What?" asked Joan.

"That James and Stacy had a huge fight the night before the murder and that he stormed out of their house and slept in his office."

"Oh, no!" cried Arliss, lifting herself up on an elbow.

"The police don't know this?" asked Joan, hand to mouth.

"I don't think he told them," replied Pamela. "He probably shouldn't either."

"No!" agreed Joan. She tapped the toe of her shoe rapidly on Pamela's tile floor.

"But he did tell them that the reason he rushed home that afternoon was because Stacy called him and begged him to come home immediately," added Pamela.

"But why would she do that?" asked Arliss, lifting herself up even more. "I thought they said she called 911 and claimed her husband was trying to break in."

"She did," said Pamela, "but according to James, she also called him at the rally and begged him to come home—which he did. That's when he found her dead."

"She called him to come home and she called 911 to report he was trying to break in?" asked Joan. "That's certainly contradictory."

"I know," agreed Pamela. "Unfortunately, 911 has the actual recording of Stacy's call to them, but James's cell phone records just indicate that a call was made from Stacy to James's cell—not what she said. As far as the police are concerned, Stacy might have called James to order him to stay away."

"Do you think maybe she changed her mind?" asked Arliss, plopping back down on the cushion of the sofa.

"You mean, she calls James at the rally and begs him to come home and then, decides that's a bad idea and calls 911 and reports him? Or she calls James and asks him to come home—and then when he shows up, she calls 911? Maybe it was her plot to ruin him because they'd fought the previous night?" surmised Joan.

"If it was, it worked," noted Pamela. "But it's a pretty elaborate plot to ruin your husband that involves your own death. And, besides, if it was Stacy's plot, then who killed her?"

"It sure seems like this Stacy woman," said Arliss, now on her elbow again, "is one confused woman. First, she wants her husband to come home, and then when he shows up, she calls 911 to report him!"

"Tell me!" agreed Joan, nodding.

"I've fought with Rocky before, and once I even kicked him out of the bedroom and made him sleep on the couch," admitted Pamela, "but I've never done anything so inconsistent as this."

"I can't imagine getting that mad at Bob," sighed Arliss. Even in her state of advanced pulchritude, Arliss didn't connect her present discomfort with the original cause of it. Maybe, thought Pamela, when Arliss was in labor, Bob might experience a smidgen of his wife's wrath.

"What are you thinking, Pamela?" asked Joan.

"I'm not totally certain," responded Pamela, rocking back and forth in her desk chair. "But there's something strange going on. I'm not sure it's anything I can ferret out, but as you two have just observed, Stacy Grant's behavior just prior to her murder—that is, the two phone calls she made—if indeed she made two phone calls—are mysteriously contradictory. It would really help if we could listen to both of them and see if we can determine which of them represents a more accurate picture of what Stacy was saying, or how they were connected, but apparently we can't. We only have

James's word as to the existence and nature of her call to him. We do, however, have a complete record of Stacy's call to 911. Maybe we can piece together a better picture of Stacy Grant and just what happened to her that day."

"You're not kidding," offered Arliss, lifting her head from the sofa.

"And I'm not just talking about her death," said Pamela finally.

"Come on, Moby Dick," said Joan to Arliss, rising and pulling on Arliss's sleeve. "Let's let Miss Marple get back to work on her sleuthing." Arliss lifted her rotund tummy carefully from the deep cushion.

"You're quite literary today, Joan," replied Pamela with a smirk. "And which fictional character are you?"

"Me? I'm Scarlett O'Hara!" She gave an expansive gesture and a deep curtsey, then turned and sauntered out the office door. Arliss waddled behind her with a bewildered shrug.

Chapter Sixteen

"WRER, may I help you?"

"Yes," replied Pamela. "I'd like to talk to Ginger Cooper, if I may."

"May I say who's calling?" asked the operator.

"Um, my name is Pamela Barnes—Dr. Pamela Barnes at Grace University—the Psychology Department. I'd like to talk to Miss Cooper about the James Grant murder case."

"Oh, Dr. Barnes," said the station operator, "just one moment. I'll check to see if she's in her office." The line switched to pre-recorded music of the blandest variety. Pamela listened as she drummed her finger tip on her desk.

"Ginger Cooper speaking. Dr. Barnes?" said a sprightly voice that she immediately recognized as the television news reporter.

"Yes, Miss Cooper," replied Pamela. "I'm not sure if you can help me, but I decided I'd ask anyway. If not, just say so. I've been volunteering on James Grant's campaign recently and his lawyer Martin Dobbs . . . ."

". . . . and his campaign manager," added Ginger Cooper.

"Uh, yes. Martin asked me to help with James's defense—if I could. I . . . visited James in the jail yesterday and I've been considering some of the things I discussed with him."

"How can I help, Dr. Barnes?" asked Ginger. "You aren't, by the way, oh, you must be . . . . the Pamela Barnes who helped the police solve that disc jockey murder a few years ago?"

"That's me," she replied sheepishly. "Anyway, I was wondering if it would be possible to get any b-roll of Stacy Grant? I mean, she was an assistant district attorney. Surely, your station has some footage of her speaking at a trial or to the press—even if it's just a tiny segment."

"B-roll, Dr. Barnes?" queried Ginger Cooper with a chuckle. "I didn't know you academics could spout our lingo. But, hey, I can probably dig up some b-roll of Stacy Grant. Might take me some time—and I'm really busy right now what with her husband's trial and all . . . ."

"That would be wonderful," Pamela said, "and all I actually need is the audio. As you probably know, that's my area—the sound part. If you could have one of your technicians dub it into an audio file—they could just email it to me as an attachment."

"Sure," she agreed. "Doesn't sound too hard. As a matter of fact, I have one of your Grace students working for me as an intern here this summer. I'll put him to work on it—a nice little assignment."

"Wonderful!" cried Pamela. "I really appreciate this."

"Does this mean, Dr. Barnes, that if you get this b-roll audio of Stacy Grant you're going to be able to exonerate her husband?"

"Oh, really, I don't know about that . . . ." Pamela laughed.

"I hope you do," observed Ginger Cooper. "Impartial press aside, Dr. Barnes, Hap Brewster is a virulent plague in this town. We all had such high hopes for James Grant. If there's a chance that Grant's innocent and can come back and give Brewster a run for his money, you'll get all the cooperation you want from me. Off the record, of course."

"Thank you, Miss Cooper," said Pamela.

"Ginger."

"Ginger."

"I'll be in touch," said the reporter and the line went dead. However, it rang almost immediately as she put the receiver in the cradle.

"Hello," she said, thinking it was Ginger Cooper again with some additional piece of information.

"Dr. Barnes?" said a strange male voice.

"Yes," she replied.

"Dr. Pamela Barnes?" asked the voice again.

"Yes."

"Dr. Barnes, don't visit James Grant any more. Stay away from him and his campaign manager Martin Dobbs. Do you understand?"

"What?" she asked, startled. Surely this was a prank call.

"You heard me."

"What did you say?"

"Stay away from James Grant and Martin Dobbs or you will be sorry." The line went dead.

"Oh, my goodness," she said to herself with a shiver. That was a threat—a genuine threat. Her immediate reaction was to call Rocky and cry and have him rush down to her office and enfold her in his arms. Her second, more logical reaction, was to call the police and report the call. Of course, she knew that the police would probably demand that she do just what the caller had demanded—but for different reasons. Even so, after hesitating for only a few minutes, she phoned the one person whom she knew would take this call seriously.

"Detective Shoop, please," she said to the operator.

"One moment," replied the police operator.

"Shoop," said the curt voice.

"Detective Shoop," she began, "this is Pamela Barnes."

"Dr. Barnes," replied the man, his relaxed voice calming her over the telephone wires. "What can I do for you? Is there something you forgot to tell me at our meeting the other day?"

"Meeting, Detective?" she asked skeptically. "No, nothing. I'm calling to report a threatening phone call that I just received."

"What did they say?" he asked, now all business.

"He—and I believe it was a he, but not a voice I recognized—said to stay away from James Grant and Martin Dobbs or that I would be sorry."

"Hmm," replied Shoop. "Very interesting. I assume you won't be following the caller's orders?"

"You know me well, Detective," she said. "But I have to admit I'm frightened. I've never received a threatening call before, although there was that time that someone tried to run me off the road . . . ."

"Tell you what, Dr. Barnes," he offered. "I'll assign a patrol car to check on your home. Also, do this for me; if you plan to meet again with Grant or Dobbs, can you let me know?"

"I can," she agreed, "but Detective, what do you think this means? If someone feels threatened just by me seeing James or Martin, doesn't that suggest that they fear I'll discover something that might implicate them in Stacy Grant's murder?"

"Not necessarily," he replied. "They just might want to be sure that Grant doesn't get out of jail before the election and they don't want anyone—you included—making waves that might upset the apple cart before the big vote."

"I suppose," she sighed, "but this seems much more personal. Someone is worried—scared even, and if they're afraid of me, then what they're covering up isn't buried very deep. You need to get your people on this, Shoop! I mean, it seems obvious to me that James Grant has been set up and someone is worried that I'll find out who. They're running scared—and you need to nab them!"

"Dr. Barnes," he scoffed, "nab them? You're getting carried away. Please, just stick to academic research—and let the police do the detecting."

"I would—if they did!" she cried. "But I can't see that any of you or your department are doing much of anything."

"Dr. Barnes," he said calmly, "we work in mysterious ways. Just because you don't see our efforts—or just because I don't report each of our moves to you directly, doesn't mean that your police department is not hard at work to keep you safe." He gave a smug little laugh.

"I hope you are, Shoop," she said with a huff, "and I'm counting on you to keep me safe. Oh, and, Shoop, please don't tell my husband about this threatening call."

"Of course not, Dr. Barnes," he replied gallantly. "I know how volatile your husband can get."

"He does not get volatile!" she exclaimed. "He's merely concerned about my welfare."

"And rightly so, if I may add," said Shoop. "I have great admiration for your long-suffering mate, Dr. Barnes."

"You make it sound as if it's a chore being married to me," she smirked.

"If you say so, Dr. Barnes," he answered.

"Whatever," she huffed. "Anyway, I just wanted to report that call. Good bye."

"Good-bye, Dr. Barnes," he said sweetly and hung up.

"The gall of that man," she said to herself with fury. He was always incredibly polite when he wanted something, but when she was asking him for a favor, he used it as an opportunity to grind salt into her wounds. Like he had some macho bond with Rocky, both of them commiserating together over having to deal with her foolhardy, misguided crime-fighting adventures.

How demoralizing this day had become. She didn't feel she was getting anywhere in helping James Grant, but somebody evidently did. Somebody must believe she was getting close enough to something that they felt the need to threaten her to stay away from James and Martin. Does that mean they were threatened by her calling Martin? She wondered. Or just showing up at the jail? That was probably where she was observed by the caller. She needed to contact Martin and tell him about the call—not because she was frightened—but because it was a sign that they were on the right track. She lifted her phone again, but just then, her computer mail message beeped. Checking her inbox, she discovered that she had a message with an attachment from

WRER. Could it be that Ginger Cooper's assistant had found some b-roll audio of Stacy Grant this soon? She clicked on the message which cryptically noted "per your request" and was signed "Eric Lundmyer—Assistant to Ms. Cooper." She opened the attachment and discovered that it was an audio file which she uploaded immediately into her acoustic analysis program. The file was quite short—maybe twenty or thirty seconds. Not a lot to go on, but certainly better than nothing.

She hit the "play" button and the pleasant voice of a woman said, "Your Honor, the District Attorney's office intends to show that the defendant, Potter Fitts Incorporated, has systematically discriminated against minorities in their hiring policies—resulting in over three hundred qualified applicants being denied employment. This unlawful discrimination has gone on at the Potter Fitts plant for over ten years. The prosecution alleges that the company's owner and founder, Potter Fitts, established these policies and maintains them today despite requests and demands from the EEOC. We ask that relief and appropriate compensation be provided to all applicants at Potter Fitts included in this suit who were not hired. We also ask that Potter Fitts define and establish a new hiring policy to be implemented within the next five months and that said policy be first approved by Your Honor."

The audio ended there. If there was any additional vocal input for Stacy Grant, it was not on the email attachment. It actually didn't matter, because this audio segment was more than sufficient for what she had in mind. She played the snippet several more times, attempting to get a good sense of Stacy Grant's voice. She realized, of course, that the way a person might speak in a formal situation, such as a courtroom, might vary dramatically from how they might sound in a tense, life-threatening situation. Even so, Stacy Grant should still sound like Stacy Grant in both instances.

Leaving the acoustic segment from Stacy Grant's courtroom presentation open on her computer software program's visual output line, she dragged her cursor down her files until she came to the file of Stacy's 911 call. She clicked on this file and pasted it into the second line of her software program, directly below the courtroom line. She then clicked on the 911 call line to refresh her mind about the sound of Stacy's voice in that instance. Here again she heard, "My husband . . . outside . . . trying to . . . break in. Please help!" The two voices certainly sounded alike. She focused on the second line—the one from the 911 call first, only because she had fewer vowels to choose from in that line. She selected the "ai" sound in the second syllable of "outside." Using her software to expand the vowel so she could see how Stacy produced all of the formants in that sound, she also selected a comparable vowel from the courtroom speech, in this case the "ai" sound in the second syllable of "denied." After a few seconds of working her magic, she was able to visually superimpose one vowel sound over the other. There was no question—the vowels were the same. That is, they were produced by the same speaker. If Stacy Grant had given that courtroom speech—and there was no reason to believe she hadn't—then it was clear that she had also been the one whose voice was on the 911 call made shortly before her murder.

Pamela was relieved but also disappointed. A small part of her had hoped that possibly it was not Stacy Grant who had called 911. She didn't know how that would have been possible, but apparently, the voice on the 911 tape was the genuine Stacy Grant. She must have called 911 because somehow she was scared that her husband—her husband who had admitted having a horrific fight with her just the night before—was trying to break into their house. Had she locked him out because of their fight? Was she that frightened? Had she told him not to come home? According to James, she had called him and begged him to come home. Or was James lying about that call? The second acoustic line on her computer screen indicated that Stacy Grant was frightened enough of her husband trying to get into their house that she called 911. What else could it possibly be?

Pamela rushed out of her office and next door to Willard Swinton's office. His door was open but Willard was not in.

She knew that Willard would not leave his office unlocked (none of the faculty did) for long. She walked to the end of the second floor hallway and looked around. At that moment, Willard appeared from the men's restroom at the far end, leaning on his cane, heading back in her direction. She stood smiling at him until he finally looked up and noticed her waiting for him at the end of the hall.

"Pamela," he greeted her, his round forehead gleaming, "a man can't even zip to the bathroom without all the women chasing him down?"

"Willard," she said, shaking her head and laughing, "I need your input now! I've got a recording of Stacy Grant speaking in court and I'm trying to compare it to her 911 recording."

"Let's take a look!" he said gleefully. They walked slowly because Willard's movements were curtailed by his use of the cane. He'd had hip surgery several years ago and had never quite recovered. Even with obvious pain when he walked, she had never heard him complain. When they got to Pamela's office, she steered him to a chair beside her computer where he sat with some difficulty.

"Listen," she said to him, sliding into her desk chair, as she played the top line. "That's the court speech. Now, here's the 911 call." She played it.

"Very similar," he said nodding.

"I did a comparison of the "ai" vowel in both selections. You can see it here." She pointed to two graphics of similar looking shaded squares.

"Identical," agreed Willard. "I don't see any problem, my dear. It appears that the 911 call is truly from Stacy Grant. But did you think otherwise?"

"I was hoping that maybe it was a setup," she explained. "You know, maybe Stacy didn't make the call and somebody else faked her voice."

"But why?" he asked.

"I don't know," she said, "but it seems all too pat that James arrived and discovered her body at almost the same moment the police arrived. And that wouldn't have happened if not for the 911 call."

"I know," he replied, "but this surely indicates that she called 911 because James was there. That 911 call seems to show that she was scared of him."

"That's what it appears," said Pamela. "But what if that wasn't what happened?"

"How?" asked Willard. "You just proved yourself that the voice on the 911 recording is the real Stacy Grant, so obviously she made the call which confirms that she was scared of her husband."

"Yes, Willard," replied Pamela, looking to her friend. His eyebrows were squeezed together with an almost ferocious intensity. It was obvious that he was as mystified as she. "But when I visited James in jail the other day, he told me that his wife—Stacy—called him and begged him to come home. That would have been about the same time as this 911 call, maybe a bit before. He and Stacy had had a fight the night before, and James had spent the night in his office, so when she called him, sounding agitated, he rushed home right away."

"Do you have a recording of that call, Pamela?" asked Willard with sudden glee.

"Unfortunately, no," she replied, despondent. "It wasn't a voice message so he didn't save it. He had no reason to. He was totally focused on getting home to her."

"So, of course," noted Willard in his rational manner, "the police believe that he's lying about this call."

"Yes," replied Pamela, "but my instinct tells me he's telling the truth. He seems as totally confused about everything that happened as we are."

"Yes," said Willard, nodding, and grabbing the mouse from Pamela so he could examine the acoustic output himself. "It doesn't really make any sense for him to do what he did. He seemed to have everything going for him. And then to just throw it all away?"

Willard clicked on the top line and played a short segment of the court room speech and then jumped to the 911 speech and replayed it. He reviewed segments of both of Stacy Grant's vocal examples, listening to one—then the other. Pamela listened with him, trying to be observant of any small detail that she might have missed.

"Hmm," he said to himself, continuing to nod. Pamela wondered what he was thinking, but she remained quiet, allowing him to formulate whatever hypothesis he could. Eventually, he asked her, "Is it possible to get any more of the court sample, do you think?"

"Can you tell me what you're looking for?" she asked.

"I'm not sure, my dear," he replied. "There is something strange about the 911 recording and I know we can't get any more of it—obviously. I was thinking that if we could get more samples of Stacy Grant's voice—possibly in other contexts?"

"I got this from WRER," said Pamela, "I'll just call back and tell them I need more examples of Stacy Grant speaking. This is her speaking in court. I'm guessing if the station has this, they surely have her in other contexts. TV stations virtually never throw away b-roll. They never know when it'll come in handy sometime in the future."

"Wonderful," said Willard. "Let me know when you have it, my dear. In the meantime, I'm going to look into some ideas I have and I'll get back to you."

"What are you thinking, Willard?"

"I'd rather not say right now," he replied. "It's rather far-fetched." With that, he lifted his large body with his ivory-handled cane and bid her *adieu* with a saucy salute and then headed out of her office and the few steps down the hallway to his own.

"What could you be thinking, Willard?" she mused to herself. "I don't know, but I've got enough to concentrate on."

Chapter Seventeen

She listened to both recordings many more times before giving up and heading home for the day. She wondered what Willard thought he noticed in the recordings that she evidently wasn't picking up. The incontrovertible truth was that Stacy Grant appeared to be the speaker on both tapes. Pamela had done as Willard had requested and called Ginger Cooper to ask for additional b-roll of Stacy Grant. The reporter had not been in her office, so Pamela had left a message and she didn't anticipate receiving a reply until at least the next day.

With a sigh, she gathered her belongings, locked her office door, and headed out into the hallway. She passed several students on their way to class and she greeted them. Both Joan and Willard were not in their offices. Stopping by the main office before heading out to her car in the parking lot (she had arrived early enough today to get a good spot), she looked in her cubby hole which was empty. Jane Marie was still stationed at her desk and the cheerful secretary waved her a greeting.

"Have you been to visit the baby chinchillas, Dr. Barnes?" she asked. "They're much cuter today than they were the other day."

"No, Jane Marie," she replied. "I've unfortunately been much too busy to check on the Green Acres gang." Jane Marie giggled. "Are you still trying to help James Grant get out of jail?"

"A number of us are," she said. "Dr. Bentley was involved in his campaign and James's law partner and lawyer,

Martin Dobbs, asked us both to assist where we could. Dr. Swinton has his fingers in this too. So it's not just me."

"Half the department seems to be rallying behind the guy," she sighed. "I wish Dr. Marks wasn't so beholden to Mrs. Brewster. He thinks the sun rises and sets on her. There's no way he'd even consider supporting Mr. Grant."

"Does he know about your feelings?" asked Pamela, looking pointedly at the young office worker. "I remember you saying how concerned your husband was that Hap Brewster would be re-elected if James wasn't exonerated soon."

"I try to keep my political views to myself, Dr. Barnes," whispered Jane Marie. "Dr. Marks is a very fair boss, but he's totally one-track minded when it comes to Katherine Brewster. It's not so much her husband, I think, but her. Hap Brewster is just part of the package."

"Mitchell doesn't have to support James," Pamela said. "It's a free country."

"I'm surprised he hasn't strong-armed you to stay out of it," whispered Jane Marie, bending over her desk and directing her comment at Pamela's ear. "If he knew that you were involved in trying to clear Mr. Grant—or if he knew that Dr. Bentley and Dr. Swinton were involved–I'm afraid he'd be furious."

"Then, please don't tell him," Pamela said. "I certainly won't."

"Don't tell him what?" asked Mitchell, opening the door to his office just as Pamela spoke this last comment. "If it's something you don't want Jane Marie to tell 'him,' I'm guessing the 'him' is me. Right?" He stood inside the doorway, his arms pressed against the jamb.

"Good lord, Mitchell," Pamela inhaled. "You scared me to death!"

"You two shouldn't be gossiping if you don't want me to listen in. The walls aren't that thick, you know!"

"Jane Marie was not gossiping," said Pamela to her boss, who eyed her skeptically with his blue eyes glaring.

"Out with it, JM," he ordered, turning to his secretary and running a hand through his thick wavy blonde hair. "What's the big secret about me?"

"Oh, Mitchell," continued Pamela, feeling incredibly guilty that she had possibly incriminated the young secretary. "It's not about you. I was just asking Jane Marie, about Katherine Brewster. I was curious about her relationship with her husband."

"And Jane Marie is supposed to know about that?" he chuckled. "And that's something you two have to keep quiet from me?"

"You are wining and dining the woman for contributions, aren't you?" asked Pamela.

"Not really. She's very generous without any persuasion on my part," he said. "And, she says virtually nothing about her husband when she comes to visit."

"And what does your wife say about all these visits, Mitchell?" asked Pamela.

"My wife? Oh, for god's sake, Pamela!" he laughed. "Velma has known about Katherine Brewster's contributions to our department for years. I guarantee you she has nothing to fear."

"I don't know," said Pamela, shaking her head. "Katherine Brewster is very attractive!"

"You two!" he huffed. "You're being ridiculous. Get back to work, both of you!" He grimaced and turned back into his office, shutting the door behind him.

"Nicely deflected, Dr. Barnes," said Jane Marie with a high-five to Pamela.

"I just turned the tables. Given Mitchell's proclivities . . . ."

"You knew he would assume that we were gossiping about him and Katherine Brewster as a possible romantic item," said the secretary.

" Little does he know," chuckled Pamela.

"Dr. Barnes! I just thought . . . what if Katherine Brewster was having an affair and her husband found out? What if she was having an affair with James Grant?"

"What?" exclaimed Pamela in astonishment. "I think that's highly unlikely, Jane Marie."

"You said yourself how attractive she is—and really, Hap Brewster isn't very attractive at all. Why would a woman as lovely as Katherine Brewster agree to marry someone as repugnant as Hap Brewster?"

"Ummm, I'm thinking, for power and money," replied Pamela. "He's the mayor and he's rich."

"Maybe Katherine Brewster killed Stacy Grant because she wanted her out of the way so she could get her husband."

"If that were true, then why would she set up James for the murder? Because if James is innocent, that's what someone did. If Katherine Brewster loved James, she wouldn't arrange things so that he'd be found with his wife's dead body. Now would she?"

"I guess not," replied Jane Marie, leaning against the top of her keyboard, arms crossed in a forlorn pose. "I wish I could figure these things out like you do."

"I wish I could figure these things out like I do too, Jane Marie." She waved goodbye and headed out of the main office, down the hallway, and out the side entrance into the parking lot.

She almost bumped into Joan who was entering from the lot.

"Pamela," Joan said, breathless, grabbing Pamela's shoulder, "I'm glad I caught you before you headed home."

"You're coming back to work this late?" asked Pamela.

"It's my night graduate class," said Joan. "How did your meeting go with James at the jail? Martin wants us all to meet—at his office."

"When?"

"Tomorrow at four. Is that okay for you? I didn't think you had class that late."

"No, I don't. I'll see if Willard can come too. He's been helping with some things and he has some ideas."

"Great," replied Joan. "Do you know where their office is?"

"On Crawford, isn't it? I've driven by and seen all the banners for James."

"That's the place," agreed Joan. "Martin will bring sandwiches, so tell your beloved not to cook tomorrow night."

"Can do," she said. "See you tomorrow."

She hopped in her little blue Civic and headed home.

Chapter Eighteen

Sleep was elusive.   Pamela tossed and turned as she mentally reviewed all of the various pieces of information she had collected that related—or more likely—didn't relate to James Grant's murder case.   What was fact?   What was supposition?   She rolled over again, trying to find a more comfortable position, growling uncontrollably when she discovered that most of the covers were embedded under Rocky's torso.   She gave a polite tug in an attempt to secure her portion of the sheets.

"What's going on?" he grumbled, rolling over and facing her. "Can't sleep?"

"No," she replied.   She felt guilty for waking him.   They had already discussed the case at supper and more hashing it out would probably not help her figure things out.   Also, she hadn't informed her husband about the threatening phone call she had received, because she knew that if he knew that her life was potentially in jeopardy, he would envelope her like a butterfly in a cocoon and never let her out of his sight.   Even so, she appreciated his insight and enjoyed using him as a sounding board to test her theories.

"Okay," he sighed, propping himself up on his elbow, "let's have it."

"I don't want to bother you; you need your sleep."

"Which I won't get with Hurricane Pamela rolling through our bed at 50 miles an hour."

She gave him one of her looks and scooted up against the headboard, knees enfolded with her hands.

"I've been going over the facts of the case," she said simply. "And the facts indicate rather obviously that James Grant killed his wife."

"Case closed," he huffed, and rolled over.

"Rocky!" she cried.

"Oh, all right!" he said. "You were never one to let facts stand in your way." He rolled back over to her and positioned his head on his hand.

"It's just that the facts are so obvious, it really looks like a set-up. I mean, if a man is going to kill his wife, why would he bash her over the head then just sit there by the body trying to revive her until the police arrive. It seems far more likely to me—and I would think to any reasonable person—that James probably accidentally walked into his house right after the murder, saw his dying wife, and stricken with grief, tried to revive her—totally oblivious of the arrival of the police."

"He didn't call the police. Or, at least there doesn't appear to be a record of him calling 911. If he really cared about the wife, wouldn't he call 911?"

"Maybe he didn't have time," she responded, turning to him. "If he just found her, he probably attempted to revive her before he even thought to call for help."

"All the more reason to make it seem like a set-up—." She paused. "The police certainly arrived at the most inauspicious moment—at least for James."

"But they were just responding to his wife's 911 call," he added.

"If it was Stacy's call," she said cryptically, with a devious look.

"What?" he exclaimed. "They've been playing that call all over the news, Pammie!"

"I know. I know," she agreed. "I haven't quite figured it out, but there's something odd about that call."

"What? Did someone else make that call?" he asked.

"I wish," she replied. "It would certainly steer the police in a different direction if not totally absolve James. But unfortunately, Willard and I have examined the voice on that

911 call from here to Sunday and it does appear that it belongs to Stacy Grant."

"So, she made the call which implies that she was frightened that her husband was trying to break into their house. Why would that be?"

"Evidently, they had fought the night before," she said. "But James felt horribly guilty about that. Particularly that Stacy died before they had made up."

"So it's possible that she was still mad at him—or even scared. Maybe she really was frightened that he might break in. You know, if they fought and she told him to get out. Then the next day he comes back. She locks the door and when he shows up, she thinks he might try to break in. Maybe that's why she called 911. Maybe he acted really threatening outside. You know, screaming at her, ordering her to let him in. We don't know."

"But, Rocky," she pleaded, "you're making all your assumptions from the point of view that Stacy's 911 call is genuine."

"Yeah?"

"Just humor me for a moment," she suggested.

"Always delighted to humor you, Babe," he chuckled and dipped his face towards her neck in a friendly amorous advance.

"Not that type of humor," she scolded. "Look at this from James's perspective. Assume he did arrive when he said he did, after Stacy was killed. Assume he did find her dead and tried to revive her and was doing that when the police arrived and arrested him. If you look at things that way, then what do you have?"

"You have nothing," he said. "None of the facts fit his version. If you assume his story is true, then Stacy must have lied on her 911 call. And why would she do that? What motive would she have? The woman ended up dead."

"Maybe Stacy didn't lie on the 911 call," offered Pamela, with a gleam in her eye.

"You mean someone coerced her into making the call and then murdered her?" he asked.

"Maybe," she said. "But there might be other ways that allow for the evidence as we have it. A 911 call from Stacy Grant reporting her husband outside of their home trying to break in. Stacy Grant dead virtually minutes after the call. James Grant found by police over the body of his dead wife virtually minutes after that. Whatever happened that afternoon, happened fast."

Rocky's eyes lit up. "Maybe someone who looked like James was trying to break in. Stacy thought he was James and reported him. He broke in, killed her, and then ran away just before James arrived on the scene."

"Possible," said Pamela, "but it was a late afternoon in August. The sun was bright. I find it hard to believe she couldn't recognize her own husband through the window. She told the operator it was her husband trying to break in. If it was a stranger, why not just say someone was trying to break in? Why implicate her husband?"

"Maybe because someone wanted to implicate him," said Rocky. "In case James didn't show up when he did."

"That makes sense," she agreed. "How could the killer know that James would arrive when he did?"

"Didn't you say that James rushed home because Stacy called him to come home?"

"Right," she said, nodding. "Maybe the real killer forced Stacy to call James and beg him to come home right before he killed her in addition to forcing her to call 911."

"God," he said, cringing, "how gruesome."

"There are other things that I have been wondering," she added.

"Like what?"

At that moment, their doorbell rang.

"My God," she whispered. "Who could that be? It's after midnight."

The doorbell rang again—twice.

"Whoever it is, they're persistent and not going away," said Rocky, climbing out of bed and crawling into his jeans and slippers. "Probably some kids playing a prank." He grabbed a long flashlight from the end table and headed out of the bedroom. Pamela realized that Rocky intended this as not only a device for visibility but also a defensive weapon if necessary.

Pamela pulled back the covers and alighted from the bed, snatching her robe and slippers in the process. She followed her husband into the living room, remaining a discreet distance behind him. Rocky was at the front door, peeking carefully through the small glass pane near the top.

"Good lord," he exclaimed, opening the front door, then the glass storm door. "Officer, is something wrong?"

A uniformed policeman stood on the front porch. Pamela could see him from where she stood, but it was unlikely that he could see her. She didn't recognize him. *Thank goodness, it isn't Shoop.* The man had shown up unannounced on her doorstep once before when she was not presentable.

"Mr. Barnes," began the officer.

"Yes," replied Rocky, seeming somewhat off-kilter to be addressed by name.

"Is your wife Pamela Barnes?" asked the office, checking a notepad.

"Yes," said Rocky. "What's wrong?" Pamela moved closer to Rocky so that the policeman could see her standing behind her husband.

"Mr. and Mrs. Barnes," he continued. "Do you know anyone who drives a black Lexus?"

"No," replied Rocky and Pamela together. "What is this about?" asked Rocky, now becoming visibly frustrated.

"Mr. Barnes, Dr. Barnes," said the policeman, "we've been keeping your house under surveillance and there has been a black Lexus parked a few houses down from you for over two hours now. They just drove away after we drove by in our patrol car several times. I believe we scared them off. I've reported it to Detective Shoop. . . ."

"What?" cried Rocky, "Shoop? Surveillance? What's this all about?"

"Sorry, Mr. Barnes," apologized the uniformed man, with a slight grin. "I assumed you knew that we were keeping your house under surveillance. Since your wife got that threatening call. Detective Shoop's orders."

"Pamela," Rocky said turning to his wife, "did you know about this?"

"Rocky, I, uh, I did know about the surveillance," she said cringing, "but I had no idea that . . . ."

"That I'd find out!" he exclaimed, crossing his arms and glaring at her. "Were you ever going to tell me about this threatening call you received?"

"It's nothing, Rocky, really," she said with a shrug.

"Nothing," he noted, "yet we have some unidentified vehicle outside our home watching our every move!"

"Uh, Mr. Barnes," interjected the police officer, "I'm really sorry if I've caused any problem here. We're just trying to protect Dr. Barnes. It's quite possible that that Lexus was parked there for some totally innocuous reason."

"Yeah," said Rocky, "not if I know my wife, Officer."

"Anyway, sir, we'll run the plates on the car and trace the owner. And don't worry. We'll keep an eye on your place. Sorry for bothering you both so late, but I wanted to check to see if you happened to know who that car belonged to."

"We don't," said Rocky, and Pamela shook her head.

"Don't worry, Dr. Barnes, Mr. Barnes," repeated the policeman, as he put away his notepad and started to depart. "We'll be keeping an eye out."

Rocky and Pamela watched the man walk down their front sidewalk, get inside his patrol car, and leave. Then Rocky carefully closed the front door and turned to his wife.

"Pamela, Pamela, Pamela," he said, shaking his head. "Now what have you gotten yourself into?"

Chapter Nineteen

It had been a battle when she'd informed her husband that she was attending a meeting at the Grant campaign headquarters the next day. Rocky was furious. He had ranted and raved that she should stay far, far away from James Grant and anyone connected to him. Did a threatening phone call mean nothing to her? She had replied that Shoop had her back and that a patrol car would apparently be following her everywhere. She didn't believe that it would, but she said what she needed to say to appease her husband. Eventually, he relented and allowed her to go to work with the promise that she call him when she left her office for Grant headquarters and when she left the headquarters for home. Rocky wanted to be aware when she was driving because he evidently considered those moments the dangerous ones. After all, in the first case she worked on with the police, someone had tried to run her off the road and Rocky had never forgotten that.

As added protection, Willard volunteered to accompany her in her Civic to the four o'clock meeting. As he didn't live all that far from their home, Pamela could drop him off on her way home and Willard could ride shotgun (so to speak) while they were traveling to and from the meeting. When she told Rocky that he didn't need to worry because she had a seventy-some- year-old, handicapped professor protecting her while she was driving, he was not amused.

"My dear," said Willard, as he hoisted himself into the passenger side of her car, "this is ever so much more exciting than taking the bus. I really feel like a useful person."

She had told Willard about the phone call threat and he was especially solicitous.

"I only wish I had a pistol," he added. "I would wield it against your attackers should they prevent us from reaching our destination."

"Willard," she said, beaming at her dear colleague, "you are my hero. Not only do you assist me in my investigations, but you protect my well-being too!"

"If anyone should accost you, my dear," he announced, "I will boff them over the head with the head of my cane. It is metal and, although my legs are weak, I still have excellent upper body strength."

"We are a dynamic duo," she said gleefully, "that is for sure!" With a passenger on board, Pamela carefully extracted her car from the parking lot, and headed off-campus towards the downtown area. Crawford Street, she knew, was on a shady, partially, residential street, just south of the center of town.

When they arrived at the small building, she parked her Civic in a spot immediately in front of Grant campaign headquarters (and the law offices of Grant and Dobbs), and came around to assist Willard in exiting her vehicle. Joan pulled up in her Taurus soon after and parked immediately beside Pamela's car; she leaped out and came to join her two colleagues as they entered through the glass-paneled front door of the tiny office in the little strip mall. A bell tinkled as the door opened. A voice Pamela recognized as Martin Dobbs called out from somewhere further back in the building.

"Make yourselves comfortable! We'll be right there!"

The three found themselves in a small lobby. Immediately in front, was a desk, obviously a secretary's desk, but without a secretary at the moment. To the left, an open area featured some sofas and a few arm chairs. In the center of the room, a fold-up table stood surrounded by seven or eight folding chairs. The table was piled with bunting, banners, posters, staplers, boxes of tape, thumb tacks, and other campaign paraphernalia. Pamela assisted Willard over to the table where he took a seat near the door and placed his cane over the back of his chair. Pamela seated herself beside him and dropped her belongings on an armchair behind her. Joan remained standing as she walked around surveying the room. Martin Dobbs entered the room with a man Pamela didn't recognize. The newcomer had coal black hair, thick with oil and a full, thick mustache. He wore a plaid suit jacket, maybe a size too small. In his arms he held a six-pack of soft drinks.

"Hello, everyone," Dobbs said in greeting, placing a tray of sandwiches in the center of the table. "Willard, Dr. Barnes, Dr. Bentley." He and the man with the beverages both took seats across from the three newcomers. Joan followed and sat down on the other side of Willard.

"I'd like you all to meet Conrad Gates," said Dobbs. "Conrad is the investigator I hired. Conrad, these are the Grace University faculty members who have been assisting with James's defense. Dr. Barnes, Willard, uh, Dr. Swinton, and Dr. Bentley." Everyone nodded in greeting.

"I brought sandwiches and Conrad has soda pop. I wanted you all to meet each other," said Dobbs, "because I think it's possible we all have information and ideas that might benefit each other. Instead of me trying to convey what each of you knows or thinks, it just seemed better to conduct a group meeting."

"That's fine with me, Martin," agreed Willard, reaching for a small ham sandwich, "and I think that the first piece of information that must be considered—both from an evidentiary standpoint and a practical standpoint—is the threatening call that Pamela received yesterday."

"What?" cried Dobbs. "You were threatened, Dr. Barnes? I had no idea." He looked at the investigator, Conrad Gates, who honed in on Pamela with his small, beady eyes.

"Yes," she confirmed as she took one of the colas. Joan followed suit. "Someone called my office yesterday and ordered me to have nothing to do with James or you, Martin. Of course, I called the police immediately. Actually, I called

Detective Shoop, who is the police officer I've worked with in the past. He promised to have a patrol car keep an eye on my home and . . . ."

"Oh, Lord," said Dobbs, "I had no idea. This happened . . . and you . . . . still came to this meeting?"

"I won't be intimidated, Mr. Dobbs," she said firmly. She took a big gulp from her bottle in a defiant gesture, like a western gunslinger downing a shot of whiskey.

"Dr. Barnes," interjected the smaller man, Conrad Gates, his dark, straight mustache making him look very much like a 1940's private investigator, "just by showing up here today, you are putting your life on the line."

"I came with her, sir," added Willard, "and I will protect her." He glanced at Pamela, his sandwich poised at his mouth.

"Willard," said Dobbs, "I don't like the idea of either of you risking your safety just to come down here."

"As I said," repeated Pamela, "the police are keeping watch over me. I think we are relatively safe. And I think it's unlikely that anyone will try anything as long as Willard is in the car with me."

"I wouldn't count on that," noted Gates, his mustache rolling as he spoke. "Although it's a moot point at the moment, because you're here. However, I will follow you home, Dr. Barnes, when you leave, and make certain you get to your house safely."

"Thank you, Mr. Gates," she replied, "if you must."

"I'd certainly feel much better," added Dobbs, "if Conrad did that."

"Wonderful, but it's not necessary," sighed Pamela. "Now, can we get on with business?"

"Yes," agreed Joan, setting down her half-eaten sandwich on a paper plate. "It seems to me that the obvious assumption from all of this business with Pamela getting a threatening call is that someone out there is worried that she's getting too close to clearing James—which means that that person is worried that she's getting close to discovering the real killer. That means that James is innocent and the real killer is still out there."

"Now you're talking, honey!" snapped Gates out of the side of his mouth, and setting down his bottle with a bang as he seemed to appraise Joan with appreciation. "Every negative has a positive in this business. You just have to know how to look at things from a different angle."

Pamela glanced over to see if Joan would bristle at being called "honey" by the grimy little detective, but Joan smiled demurely and puffed out her chest.

"Conrad," said Dobbs with an expansive gesture of his arms, "I guess we should hand the meeting over to you." No one seemed to object, so Conrad Gates stood up and placed his hands palm down on the table.

"So," he started, referring to a hand-written list on a clipboard he had placed in front of him. "Here's what we got. James Grant, Martin Dobbs. Friends from college. Both graduate the same year from Grace University's law school and decide to form their own law firm. James marries college sweetheart Stacy Rollins, also a graduate of the law school here. She goes to work for the DA and rises through the ranks until she eventually makes assistant district attorney. Over the years, she's been involved in prosecuting some rather nasty individuals. Believe me, I'm looking into a possible connection there. At the same time, James and Martin have been successful too. Last year James begins discussing the possibility of running for mayor against longtime incumbent Hap Brewster. Martin becomes James's campaign manager and they begin a campaign in earnest. Just a few weeks ago, polls were indicating that James was actually leading Hap Brewster and it looked like he would very probably win in November—just a few months from now."

"We know all this, Mr. Gates," said Joan.

"Just a review," replied Gates, "Miss . . . uh, Dr. Bentley." He gave her a wide, infectious smile. "Anyway, last week, James was scheduled to speak at a rally in the park. This event occurred. Media covered the event. Incumbent mayor Brewster and his team arrived shortly after James spoke and hassled him in front of television reporter Ginger Cooper. Eventually, Ms. Cooper finished her post-speech interview of James and turned her attention to Hap Brewster, conducting an interview of him that lasted approximately fifteen minutes."

"Conrad," interjected Dobbs, "tell them why this is important."

"Yep," said Gates, pushing harder on the table with his hands for emphasis. He jabbed at his clipboard as he continued. "Television station WRER has a record of exactly when the interview between Ginger Cooper and Hap Brewster was conducted. And, unfortunately, it occurred at almost the exact same time that Stacy Grant called 911 and the police were dispersed to the Grant home where they found James kneeling over Stacy's body."

"Meaning," said Willard, "that it would be impossible for Hap Brewster to have killed Stacy Grant." He wiped his hands on a paper napkin.

"The wonders of accurate date and time counters on video recordings," said Gates with a shrug.

"But not impossible for one or more of his cronies to do it," noted Pamela.

"That is correct," said Gates. "The station's video counter only tells us that Hap Brewster himself could not have committed the crime. We have no idea where his various associates, such as Victor Baines and Kevin Sturges, were."

"But now that Pamela has received that threatening call," added Joan, "who else would it be but a Brewster supporter?"

"Listen," said Gates, slapping his hands on the table again. The effect was definitely gripping and each time he did it, it caused Pamela to jump in her seat. "Let's get the rest of the evidence out first and see if we can find any discrepancies before we start wondering about the 'who' in the case."

"Yes," agreed Dobbs. "Anything else that you have, Conrad?" He gathered the wrappings from the sandwiches and pushed them into a large paper bag.

"I have done a thorough background check of James, Stacy, and Martin—sorry, buddy." He glanced briefly at Dobbs with a sad hang-dog expression. "For all we know, Stacy may have been killed for reasons unrelated to the election. Unlikely, but possible. I'm looking into everything. But so far I haven't found a connection. So, why don't you academic folks tell me what you've got, okay?"

"Go ahead, Pamela," said Willard.

"Yes, Pam," agreed Joan. "Tell Mr. Gates what you're thinking and what you found." Joan gazed at Gates with a shy smile.

"I haven't really found anything specific," Pamela said, sheepishly, "but I have some thoughts. Willard too. Right away, we were both curious about the 911 recording. It seemed strange to both of us, although we're not exactly certain why. At one point, I thought the voice on the tape might not be Stacy Grant. I asked Ginger Cooper at WRER to send me some audio samples of Stacy's voice in other circumstances—which she did. I then compared the two samples—hoping to find that the 911 caller was someone other than Stacy—but it wasn't."

"Yet, you still believe there's something strange about the 911 call?" asked Gates.

"Yes, I do," said Pamela.

"Dr. Barnes," said Gates, bending over the table and giving her a penetrating stare, "I want you to keep examining those recordings. You too, Dr. Swinton. If you see any discrepancy, no matter how small, let me know."

"We will," agreed Willard, riveted to Gates and nodding with enthusiasm.

"This case is a lot like one I worked a few years back," continued Gates. "Poor schmuck was discovered with his wife's dead body. This one happened outside. They'd been boating and he claimed his wife fell overboard and he jumped in to save her. He managed to drag her to shore and tried to resuscitate her but it was too late. Police hemmed and hawed. Couldn't decide whether to charge him or not. I mean, the fact that he dragged her in and tried to save her looked good, but when they checked further, it turned out the couple had been fighting. In fact, the wife had contacted an attorney about filing for divorce. No one knows why they were out boating together. Neither one of them had any real interest in the sport. The police eventually arrested him, claiming that he set up the boating excursion to cover the murder attempt. No eye witnesses. He could have pushed her over and held her under water until she drowned and then dragged her to shore and pretended to try to revive her."

"Didn't the coroner find any suspicious marks on the wife's body?" asked Dobbs. "I mean, if the husband held her underwater, you'd think she'd try to fight him off."

"The coroner's report was inconclusive," replied Gates. "There were marks, but the coroner said they were also consistent with marks the husband might have made dragging her to shore."

"There's nothing like that in James's case," said Joan. "I don't see how hitting someone over the head with a candlestick from behind would give the victim a chance to leave any defensive marks."

"It wouldn't," replied Gates. "But the police can surmise a number of clues about the killer from the head wound."

"Such as?" asked Willard.

"This is conjecture on my part," noted Gates, "because they obviously believe they've got their man, but killing someone by hitting them on the head with a metal object supposes fairly good upper body strength."

"Something you have, Willard," said Pamela with a chuckle.

"Yes," he replied. "It's gratifying to know I could do in a poor, defenseless woman."

"It also presupposes that the killer attacked from behind because the wound was on the back and side of her head. Which also suggests that Stacy knew the killer as she was apparently willing to turn her back on him—or her."

"Could it have been a her?" asked Pamela.

"It would have to be a very strong woman," said Gates, "if it was—and probably a tall one. Or Stacy would have had to be seated with her back to the killer."

"Any number of possibilities that could have occurred," said Dobbs. "What about how the killer arrived? Or why? Is it possible that Stacy mistook the real killer for her husband when she called 911? She might have seen the killer outside."

"So she let him in and then turned her back on him so he could bash her over the head?" posited Gates. "Doesn't sound likely."

"You are all aware that James says he received a call from Stacy urging him to come home at once," said Pamela.

"Yes," agreed Martin. "He did, but unfortunately there is no recording of it. I've checked with the police and they admit that there was a call made to James' cell shortly before the 911 call from the Grant landline phone. But their belief is that it was Stacy trying to contact her husband when she saw him attempting to break into their home. Possibly they argued. But whatever occurred during that short call, the police believe that it was enough to frighten Stacy into then phoning 911."

"So without the actual content of the call from Stacy," argued Gates, "it looks really bad for James."

"He did tell me when I saw him," continued Pamela, "that the call from Stacy was very short. In fact, she didn't even let him ask her any questions or even respond. She just told him to come home and then she hung up."

"That doesn't seem all that strange," suggested Joan. "I mean, if she was scared that someone was trying to break in, she'd just tell him what she needed to say and then hang up."

"But, then why immediately call 911 and report James for trying to break in?" mused Willard.

"There are a number of very strange things in this case," observed Pamela, "and if you notice, they all concern phone calls."

"What do you mean, Pamela?" asked Dobbs.

"The phone call from Stacy to James that we don't have, the phone call from Stacy to 911 that we do have. If you think about it, these two calls cancel each other out. If the police had a recording of the first, they would suspect the validity of the second. But they only have the second, so they have no reason to believe the first even exists."

"Whereas, we, on the other hand," said Gates, finger to mustache, "we believe in the existence of both—leaving us with the major discrepancy of this case. Which call really represented what Stacy Grant was trying to tell us? Or even, which of these calls did Stacy Grant actually make?"

"Or," said Pamela, "did she make either one of them?"

"What?" said Dobbs. "I thought you verified Stacy's voice on the 911 call, Dr. Barnes."

"I did," she replied. "But consider the repercussions if Stacy Grant hadn't made any phone calls at all."

"You mean, Pamela," said Joan, "if someone faked her voice?"

"Or something," replied Pamela. She squinted at the center of the table at the pile of leftover food and wrappings in an attempt to focus in on the answer to the puzzle.

"I don't know how we'd go about proving that," said Gates. "But if someone went to all that trouble, it indicates that someone was planning this murder for quite some time."

"I don't know if that's what happened," said Pamela. "I just know that there is something strange about the recording."

"Pamela, my dear," said Willard, nudging his colleague on the arm, "we must redouble our efforts and examine that recording with greater thoroughness."

"Yes," agreed Pamela, "we must, and we will." She smiled at Willard and then looked around the room at the three other faces looking towards them.

"Everyone," said Dobbs, eventually, "it looks like we have several new directions to try. Pamela and Willard will be checking out Stacy's 911 call. Conrad will look into Stacy and James's background to see who—if anyone—might have a reason to harm either of them. I, myself, will go see James in jail again and press him more about anything he can contribute to our efforts. And Joan, I'm sure you will help Willard and Pamela in any way possible."

"I certainly will," replied Joan.

With that, the group rose, assisting Martin Dobbs in clearing the trash from the table. Pamela and Willard headed out to her car. Joan remained behind and the last Pamela saw of her friend, she was chatting—or rather, flirting—with the team's investigator, Conrad Gates. Gates had apparently forgotten about his promise to follow Pamela home.

Chapter Twenty

Pamela drove carefully down the main street of Reardon, chatting amiably with Willard. Although she and Willard worked together closely on research studies on a fairly regular basis, their interactions were primarily professional. This car ride was a decided change in their mode of communication and Pamela was enjoying Willard's companionship as she made her way towards the small suburban apartment complex where she knew he lived alone.

"How exhilarating!" said Willard, practically beaming. "Doesn't it feel grand to be able to use our research skills to help someone in such a personal way?"

"Definitely," she replied, sending him a quick short smile so that she could keep her eyes on the road.

"Of course, my dear," noted Willard, his hand bracing himself against the dashboard, "I forget how involved you've been in helping others with your investigative powers." He gripped the top of the dash as Pamela took a sharp curve. Noticing his firm grip, she wondered if Willard had been warned about her driving skills by someone.

"It will feel especially wonderful," she said to him over her shoulder, "if we can actually figure out who really killed Stacy—assuming, of course, that James didn't."

"Oh, he didn't," said Willard, his chubby brown cheeks squishing together. "Believe me, Pamela, I have known Martin for years. And James is his closest friend. They are both honorable men. I can't imagine either of them hurting a fly, let alone a person."

"I trust your character judgment, Willard," she assured him. "We will really both have to get busy and try to figure out what it is about that recording of Stacy that makes it unusual."

"And hope that whatever it is, it will vindicate James," said Willard, tapping his cane on the floor in confirmation.

"Are we in agreement that it's definitely Stacy's voice on the 911 recording?" she asked him. She turned a second time, down a residential street where she knew Willard resided. Even though she'd never been here, she'd heard him mention his home and location and had registered where it was because it was so close to her own home.

"I would say definitely," he replied. "Oh, right here, my dear." Willard tapped at the side passenger window at a two-story red brick apartment complex with individual outside entrances for each unit. "I'm the third door down." She pulled into a space directly in front of the apartment. It was a homey, well-kept unit with a white wooden porch and a porch swing. She could see several potted plants in the front window. Willard was a bachelor but obviously took pride in his residence.

"Let me help you," she said, hopping out of the car and coming around to the passenger door so she could open it for him. Willard carefully stepped out, using his cane to assist him.

"Would you care to come in, my dear?" he asked her.

"Oh, Willard, thank you," she said with unexpected embarrassment, "but it's getting late and my husband gets fussy when I return home late. He expects me to be there to eat what he cooks for me. He seems to enjoy feeding me."

"How lucky for you!" exclaimed Willard. "It must be lovely to be able to share your evening meal with someone." She felt terrible at that point and wondered if she should ask him to get back in the car and come over to her house for dinner. "Of course, I have Phoebe to share my dinner with me," he added.

"Phoebe?" she asked. Willard had never discussed his social life—if he had one. She knew he'd never been married, but he never insinuated that he was dating anyone.

"Yes," he said, using his cane to head towards the front door of his small apartment. "She demands her kitty treats by a reasonable hour or she howls all night long in protest."

"Oh, you have a cat!" said Pamela. "We have a dog!"

"They are like part of the family, aren't they?"

"Definitely!" she responded. At that, he had reached the door and opened it. Immediately a huge flash of fur zipped out and encircled his feet several times.

"Phoebe!" he scolded the cat, who immediately stopped in front of him, looking up. "Say hello to Dr. Barnes." Phoebe meowed.

"My goodness, Phoebe," said Pamela, bending over and speaking sweetly to the large feline. "You are quite the kitty! You must weigh forty pounds!"

"Yes," he said to her, "something like that. I'm afraid I'm too indulgent. I give her whatever she demands."

"I know how that happens," she said. "They can be very persistent."

"Yes, they can," he said, now standing in the doorway, facing out. Phoebe stood beside him, her giant tail flipping back and forth like a fluffy metronome.

"Willard," she said, turning to leave, "I'll see you tomorrow. We can go over the recording some more then."

"Very good, my dear," he said, with a slight wave, and then gently closed the door, encasing himself and the cat behind it.

Pamela walked back to her car and got inside. She started her engine and drove down the short street that housed Willard's apartment complex where she stopped to turn onto the more trafficked roadway. Before she could enter the road, however, a large, black car—possibly the Lexus that had been outside their home the night before—pulled directly in front of her and stopped sideways in the street, blocking her movement. Pamela was flabbergasted.

A large man got out of the car and walked with conviction towards the driver's side of her car. She immediately recognized him as Victor Baines, Hap Brewster's campaign manager. He was wearing a dark suit, totally inappropriate for this hot summer day. His red, sweaty face indicated he was annoyed and she surmised that she was partially the cause of his fury.

"Dr. Barnes," he shouted, pounding on her window. She kept the window rolled up. The man had blocked her car's movement on a public street and he seemed mad enough to harm her. She grabbed her cell phone, intent on calling the police. "I just want to talk to you, Dr. Barnes." He knocked again on the window.

"Move your car!" she shouted at him. "You're blocking my way!"

"Listen, lady!" he yelled through the closed window. "I'm trying to be polite."

"Polite people don't block the street and keep drivers from moving!"

"I don't have anything against you, lady," he continued, his large belly protruding from his tightly buttoned suit jacket. "I just want to warn you that you don't know what you're getting into."

"What I'm getting into?" she yelled back at him. She held up her cell phone. "Get out of my way or I'll call the police."

"That's not necessary!" he screamed. "I'm leaving. I just want you to know how foolish you are to be mixed up with James Grant and his group. He killed his wife. Why not just leave things alone?"

"You mean why not just let Hap Brewster get re-elected?" she cried back.

"An accused killer can't run for—or be elected–to anything."

"He can if he's exonerated."

"That's not going to happen, lady!" screamed Baines, his red face getting a deeper shade of red, sweat pouring off of his forehead. "Just leave it alone!" he repeated.

"Or what?" she asked, bravely—more bravely than she felt. The pane of glass between them was little comfort if the large man decided to pick up a stone or even his shoe and smash it.

"I'm just trying to reason with you," he cried, clinging onto the top of her window with his fingertips. "You've been involved in other murder investigations and some reporter seeing you messing around in this one is liable to think there's some wild chance that Grant's innocent."

"He is!" she yelled.

"He isn't," retorted Victor Baines, extracting a cloth hanky from his suit coat jacket and wiping the flood of sweat from his brow. "But with you prancing around the edges, people will think he is!"

"So what?" she replied, shaking her head. The man appeared desperate, almost to the point of passing out. "Can't Hap Brewster compete fairly against a reputable opponent?"

"If you'd just stay out of it, he wouldn't have to!" replied Baines, panting in the hot late afternoon sun. "Justice would take its course, Grant would be convicted, and we'd have a nice election with no controversy."

"You mean, you'd have an election with no opposition," she shot back. "Look, I know Hap Brewster has run in every election unopposed. Or with minimal opposition. This is probably a new situation for him—for you."

"Lady, Hap has been mayor of Reardon for longer than you've probably been alive."

"So, don't you think it's time for a change?" she asked sweetly as she rolled down the window a crack. "Mr. Baines, you look ill. I recommend you get out of the sun and take off that suit coat and tie. That is, after you move your car!" Victor Baines took another wipe of his forehead with his hanky and then deposited it in his pocket. Lifting himself with difficulty from the side of her car, where he'd propped himself, he trudged over to his car and got inside. She watched him fiddle with the dashboard for a minute—probably adjusting the air conditioning upward. Then, with a lurch, he abruptly turned the wheels and rolled out into the main street traffic with a screeching noise.

Chapter Twenty-One

Later that night, when she was alone grading papers in her bedroom, she was able to contemplate the events of the day. She had told Rocky about the group meeting at Grant campaign headquarters because she was quite late for dinner and she had used it as an excuse—and for why she hadn't phoned him to let him know she was on her way home. Well, it was a genuine excuse, she thought, although not the only thing that delayed her return home that evening. She hadn't mentioned her run-in with Brewster henchman Victor Baines in the street. If Rocky found out about that, she'd never hear the end of it. In retrospect, the event sounded worse than it probably was, she thought. A big, burly guy forced her car to stop in the street, then got out and verbally threatened her at her car window. Yes, it did sound frightening, but when she replayed the confrontation in her memory, all she saw was an overweight, overwrought man out in the grueling heat who appeared about two minutes away from having a heart attack. Even so, she saw no reason to mention the brief encounter with Baines to Rocky. However, she probably should report the run-in with Baines to the police, or at least to Shoop.

She glanced down at the pile of papers on her lap. These were the students' rough drafts of their semester research projects. She knew she wouldn't finish them all in one evening. In rough draft stage, they were almost all unbearably unreadable. It was torture to get through one or two an hour. She looked at the completed ones on her hassock—maybe five if she was lucky. She bent back down to the paper in front of her. Where was Candide? Her little buddy must be snuggled up with Rocky out in the living room, she surmised. This thought caused her to remember dropping Willard off at his apartment and seeing his extremely large cat. She realized that Willard's cat probably had quite a few pounds on Candide and could probably knock her tiny poodle flat with her tail.

"Hey, Babe," called Rocky as he sauntered into their bedroom. Candide pranced along behind him. "It's getting late. Did you get many of those things read?" he asked referring to the research papers.

"Unfortunately, no," she replied. "I keep drifting off."

"Exhausting day," he noted. "That meeting must have been a doozie."

"Not really," she shrugged. "More an organizational thing. Martin introduced us to his investigator and we all sort of laid our cards on the table. Unfortunately, nobody has many cards."

"What's he like?" questioned Rocky, balancing on the hassock.

"Kind of greasy," she said, "but I guess that appeals to Joan. At least, she seemed to be flirting with him when I left."

"Does the investigator appear to know anything?" he asked.

"He's done a lot of background stuff on James and Stacy and the Brewster camp," she replied, "but he hasn't turned up anything that might help yet. You know that Stacy is . . . was an ADA. She's evidently prosecuted some pretty scruffy fellows."

"Oh, yeah. Who?"

"According to Gates—the investigator—tax evasion cases, some domestic violence, burglary. You know, the usual."

"You think this Gates guy knows what he's doing? I mean, could any of the defendants in any of her cases have come back to kill her?"

"He's still looking into that," she said. "There are quite a few cases that she prosecuted herself or assisted with. Many of those resulted in a conviction and of those who were, many of those individuals are still in jail—but some are out now. The question is if a person who was released from jail would risk getting sent back to seek revenge on the prosecutor who sent him there."

"If they're mad enough, I suppose," he said, sitting next to her on the hassock.

"Hey, don't mess up my papers!" she cried. Rocky stood up and restacked the papers.

"Sorry!" he replied. "Just wanted to get close enough to you to give you a back rub."

"Why didn't you say so, Mr. Barnes?" she asked, smiling. She set down the paper she was grading and went over to the bed, flinging herself face down on top of the covers. "Here I am. If you want to give me a back rub."

"I'll turn on the news while I work," he whispered in her ear, kneeling behind and to her side. He hit the remote button and WRER anchor Ginger Cooper appeared on screen. The sight of her reminded Pamela of their conversation and the pretty reporter's willingness to help with her investigation. Rocky's large hands kneaded Pamela's back, rubbing the kinks of the day away.

The local news contained nothing new about the Grant murder case. In a related story, however, a reporter presented a brief account that indicated that Mayor Hap Brewster had filed an injunction with the local Election Commission to have James Grant's name removed from Reardon's mayoral ballot in November.

"Oh, for heaven's sake!" mumbled Pamela, face down on the mattress as Rocky pushed and rubbed her back. "Why does that man seem to feel so intimidated by James? He's in jail, for heaven's sake! Why doesn't Brewster just let this play out? Let James stay on the ballot. Surely, if nothing happens before the election to free James, who will vote for an accused murderer? All Brewster does by forcing the issue—it seems to me—is to make voters curious why he doesn't trust them to decide for themselves."

"I agree," said Rocky, never losing the rhythm of his back rubbing strokes. "He ought to leave well enough alone."

The screen changed to commercials and the couple watched in silence as Rocky continued his efforts to relax his wife. Another slick, well-produced commercial advertising the candidacy of Hap Brewster appeared. This one was even more impressive than the short super-hero one she had seen the other day. There was documentary footage of Brewster who was made to look like a knight slaying various possible foes. A professional voice-over and an original musical score contributed to the polished effect.

"Wow!" said Rocky. "That was good. I mean, I haven't seen a political ad that well done since the Reagan 'Morning in America' one."

"Yeah," she agreed, "Not your typical used-car commercial. Even better than the one we saw yesterday. Slick." It was the only word that seemed appropriate. She was used to seeing corny ads for local political campaigns.

"It makes Hap Brewster look like a hero," noted Rocky, stopping his ministrations to her back.

"Are you done with my back rub?" she asked, turning over on her side. Rocky scooted down beside her.

"Am I?"

"It's too bad James can't get the guy who did that ad to make one for him," she sighed.

"James! James!" he said gruffly, sitting up. "For a guy you've barely met, we sure discuss him a lot!" His loud voice appeared to serve as a beacon to their dog, and Candide jumped up on their bed, looking from one of them to another.

"Candide!" she exclaimed, clapping her hands to get her pet's attention. "I met a very nice kitty today. She was much bigger than you!"

Candide lodged himself between them.

"Great!" moaned Rocky. "First James comes between us, now Candide!"

"No one is coming between us," Pamela replied to her husband, nuzzling his chin. "Did I tell you how much I loved dinner tonight?"

"Did you?"

"I did," she said in his ear.

Candide joined in and licked Rocky's other ear.

"No! Stop!" said Rocky, swatting away the dog's attention with his hand. "I'm not a meat loaf."

"You're probably covered in juices from tonight's amazing lamb stew," she observed. "Candide can't resist you any more than I can."

"You not resisting me," he whispered to her, rolling over towards her and pulling her to him. "I'd like to see that."

She traced her finger over the familiar features of her husband's face. Yes, there were a few remnants of the evening's meal still there. But more than that, there was the face she loved more than any other. His rough skin, his firm features, his tender expression. She reached out and embraced him. Candide propped himself up on Rocky's shoulder and looked into Pamela's face—only a few inches away. It was difficult, she thought, being romantic with the long black snout of a small poodle two inches from your nose. She closed her eyes. Rocky pulled her tight to his body. Her mind filled with the rich images of a political commercial—an unforgettable political commercial.

Chapter Twenty-Two

The next day, it was difficult to concentrate on her classes. Her mind kept wandering from her lecture material to the Stacy Grant murder investigation. Her students were full of questions about their upcoming research papers and with the summer session so much shorter than regular semesters, she felt she had to spend the additional time after class answering any questions they might have in order for them to complete the demanding projects on time. She now found herself standing behind the lectern in the second floor lecture hall, chatting with several students about said paper.

"So, you don't want us to give any of our own opinions in our papers?" asked one tall girl in Bermuda shorts and her hair in braids.

"No," replied Pamela, her pat answer rehearsed over many years of requiring this particular paper. "You can't use first person statements, but obviously, your paper is filled with your ideas, but you argue those ideas by supporting them with evidence and you present that evidence in third person."

"You mean," said a male student, "we can say 'voices convey personality,' but we can't say, 'I believe that voices convey personality.'"

"Something like that," noted Pamela with a chuckle at the student's simplification. The students began gathering their belongings. Pamela looked up to the back of the lecture hall and noted a woman standing hesitantly in the doorway. As the students wandered out of class, chatting and laughing, the woman entered and began walking towards Pamela. As the woman came closer, Pamela realized who she was because she had seen her leave Mitchell's office only a few days ago. This was Katherine Brewster, wife of Reardon's mayor. What was she doing here?

"Dr. Barnes?" questioned Katherine Brewster, walking down the aisle of the large classroom. "Dr. Pamela Barnes?"

"Yes," replied Pamela. What did the mayor's wife want with her?

The woman was dressed like the society queen she obviously was–wearing a magenta linen suit and a dark purple silk top. Her beige leather heels were probably designer too, reasoned Pamela. She certainly didn't own any shoes like that. Mrs. Brewster's hair was professionally coifed and her diamond earrings glistened. Her long, elegantly manicured nails indicated that this was a woman who did not do her own floor scrubbing.

"Can I help you?" asked Pamela, as the sophisticated woman stopped directly in front of the lectern.

"Dr. Barnes," began Katherine Brewster, "Dr. Marks informed me that you would be here and that your class was just concluding. I was hoping I might catch a word with you. My name is Katherine Brewster . . . ."

"Yes, Mrs. Brewster," interrupted Pamela, "I know who you are."

"Oh," responded the mayor's wife with a lilting laugh. "Possibly Mitchell–Dr. Marks–has spoken of me. But, anyway, that doesn't matter. Actually, Dr. Barnes, I've come to talk to you today to plead with you to refrain from becoming involved–or at least–any further involved in this mess with James Grant."

"What?" exclaimed Pamela. "Did your husband send you, Mrs. Brewster?"

"No, no," she said, "he would never do that. However, I am aware of what goes on in my husband's campaign, Dr. Barnes, and he is extremely concerned about all of these individuals who seem to be conspiring to aid this wife killer– and thus–damage my husband's campaign. It's incredible for me to believe that anyone in this department would be involved in such shenanigans. Excuse me for being blunt."

Pamela was speechless. Had Mitchell sent this woman to see her? Did he even know she was here and what she was demanding? Katherine Brewster stood before her, eyelids fluttering, arms crossed primly, likely anticipating that Pamela would produce an agreeable reply.

"Mrs. Brewster," she began, warmly, "I understand from Mitchell–Dr. Marks–that you have been a generous benefactress of our department, and as a member of the department, I am sincerely grateful for your contributions. However, you surely are aware that contributing money to an academic department does not allow the donor the right to dictate to individual faculty members how they should behave–with regards to the use of those funds and with regards to their own personal behavior outside of their professional duties. In other words, Mrs. Brewster, what I do on my own time is my business."

Katherine Brewster gave a small gasp and straightened her suit jacket, ostensibly to allow herself time to gather her thoughts.

"Dr. Barnes, I'm certainly not trying to order you about. It's simply that I don't understand how someone of your intelligence and professional standing–like Mitchell, Dr. Marks–would become embroiled with an accused murderer. You surely must see what such involvement does to your image in the community."

"Mrs. Brewster, I'm quite touched that you're so worried about the image of a person you don't even know. However, I'm not in the least bit concerned about my image and I don't believe that my involvement in James Grant's defense will damage it in the slightest."

Pamela was actually starting to enjoy this polite debate. She leaned over the lectern and smiled her most engaging smile at the woman.

"I-I, uh, Mitchell said you were a reasonable person," Katherine Brewster scowled, her bright red lipstick on her lower lip smearing onto her teeth as she squeezed her mouth together.

"I am," said Pamela. "Very reasonable. Just ask anyone I work with. It's that reasonableness–or you might say, reasoning—that has allowed me to help the local authorities solve several murder cases over the last few years. All I'm doing now is attempting to do the same for James."

"But that man was found standing over his dead wife!" exclaimed Katherine Brewster, diamond earrings sparkling in response.

"All the more reason for him to have people in his corner—as the police seem to have already made up their minds."

"And for good reason," Mrs. Brewster responded. She carefully brushed a wayward strand of hair from her cheek.

"Mrs. Brewster," said Pamela, "did you really think you could just walk in here and tell me to stay off James's defense team?"

"I am attempting to appeal to your good judgment, Dr. Barnes," said Katherine Brewster.

"Have you been appealing to the good judgment of all the other people assisting in James's defense?" asked Pamela.

"Uh, no," replied Mrs. Brewster, looking down. "But, Dr. Barnes, you are well known for solving several local murder cases. If people find out that you're working for James Grant, they're liable to think there's a possibility that he didn't kill his wife . . . ."

"He didn't!"

"You can't believe that!" cried Katherine.

"The more that people from your husband's campaign try to intimidate me into quitting my efforts to help James, the more . . . ."

"What people?" Brewster asked suddenly. "Has someone other than me said anything to you about this?"

"You mean your husband didn't send you here?" asked Pamela.

"No, Dr. Barnes," said the mayor's wife. "Believe it or not, this was my idea. What other people from my husband's campaign have asked you to stop helping James Grant?"

"For starters," said Pamela with a sigh, coming from behind the lectern and stepping down a level to the floor where she could face Katherine Brewster nose to nose. "For starters, your husband's right hand man, Victor Baines, stopped my car in the street yesterday and pounded on my car window demanding that I stay out of the investigation."

"He did?" she responded, seeming aghast and then as the implications set in, somewhat deflated.

"Yes," said Pamela, "and I also received a threatening phone call a few days ago. That may have been Baines, but maybe not. I don't know."

"I don't know what to say," replied the woman, noticeably shaken. She stepped over to one of the student desk chairs and collapsed into it. "Dr. Barnes, I'm really sorry. My purpose in talking to you today was to try to reason with you–not strong arm you. I had no idea that anyone from my husband's campaign had been harassing you."

"Possibly at your husband's request?" asked Pamela sitting next to her.

"Oh, no!" she cried. "I can't believe that of Harold!"

"I hope you're right, Mrs. Brewster."

"I guarantee you that I will discuss this with Harold and I will be certain he knows what Victor has done. This will not happen again."

"I would appreciate that," said Pamela, "but truthfully, Mrs. Brewster, I don't need you to fight my battles for me. All things considered, it might be best not to make waves right now."

"All right, Dr. Barnes," replied Katherine Brewster. "I am so sorry that this has happened to you. I had no idea . . . I really just thought you were a nosy busybody out to make trouble. I didn't realize that . . . Mitchell speaks so highly of you, and I think so highly of Mitchell. I have always loved this department. I was a Psych major many years ago when I was a student, did you know?"

"I believe I had heard that," said Pamela with a smile. "And Mrs. Brewster . . . ."

"Please, call me Katherine," she said warmly, a hand on Pamela's arm.

"Katherine," said Pamela agreeably, "I just don't understand why your husband is so fearful of anyone assisting James. Even if James is cleared, it doesn't mean that he'll necessarily defeat your husband. I mean, your husband has been mayor for many years. He has a loyal following, I would assume . . . ."

"Oh, he does," gushed the woman. "And you're right. Harold needn't be fearful of this Grant fellow. I mean, he's defeated many other candidates. I think it's just because Grant was running a bit ahead of Harold in the most recent polls."

"But polls change, Mrs. Brewster," said Pamela calmly. Of course, she hoped the polls remained the same if—when— James was exonerated and that he would ultimately defeat Hap Brewster, but she didn't feel the need to ram her personal viewpoint down this poor woman's demoralized throat. Even though that's exactly what Katherine Brewster had intended to do with her when she entered her lecture hall hardly thirty minutes ago.

"Anyway," said Katherine, rising and straightening her skirt, "I just wanted to stop by and speak with you. Please keep in mind what we talked about. And please take care of yourself. Victor Baines has a bark that's worse than his bite. If you must know," she confided in a whisper, "he had by-pass surgery a few years ago and he really hasn't been the same since. I can't believe he would—or could—hurt you. Harold keeps him on staff because the two of them started out together in politics. They're very close."

"I appreciate that information, Mrs. Brewster," Pamela replied, standing with her and walking her out into the hallway where they said their farewells.

Chapter Twenty-Three

After seeing Katherine Brewster off, Pamela returned to her office with relief. Opening the door of her mini-fridge, she removed her lunch sack and extracted the sandwich that Rocky had designed for her today. A wave of onion wafted through her office as she unwrapped the waxed paper around the tiny croissant, piled thick with layers of cheese, meat, and various greens. Rocky had also included some of his special granola mix which he kept in a container on their kitchen island. It was composed of various nuts, coconut, dried fruits segments, and dark chocolate chunks—which, he assured her, had no calories at all. Thank goodness, she had devised a system to keep her weight at a tolerable level. She forced herself to workout for an hour almost every morning before class at a local gym. Also, her policy for eating Rocky's marvelous cooking was one serving only—and a small portion at that. She knew she'd never be able to totally resist his delicious recipes—and she didn't. Even so, she attempted to behave with moderation in her eating habits because otherwise she would easily become a blimp as the contented wife of a gourmet cook.

She took her scrumptious-smelling sandwich to her sofa, along with her thermos which contained the remnants of some currant tea. She had managed to savor several sandwich bites when Joan and Arliss arrived at her door together.

"Oh!" exclaimed Pamela, mid-slurp, "Arliss! I haven't seen you in a while. How are the baby chinchillas doing?"

The two women moved into Pamela's office and made themselves at home in their favorite spots–Joan in the straight back chair by the door and Arliss in Pamela's rolling desk chair. Watching Arliss trying to position herself and her huge belly in the moving seat was humorous because the wheels on the chair wouldn't hold still long enough for Arliss to lower herself into the seat. She would have gladly relinquished the sofa to her very pregnant friend, but Arliss was being stoic today and not asking for favors.

"Careful, girl," noted Joan. "We don't need you and baby Goodman on the floor."

"I'm fine, Joan," retorted Arliss, panting, "I have at least two weeks to go and I just saw my OB yesterday and he says I'm right on schedule. And, Pam, Eva's babies are fine and getting bigger and cuter every day. You should come down to the lab and visit them."

"I will the minute I get a chance," responded Pamela still on her sofa, taking a bite of her sandwich. "Is Bob getting excited?"

"More than me, I'm afraid," said Arliss with a scowl. "That's all he talks about. It's not as if he hasn't seen babies being born before. I mean, we have Eva now—and our monkey Bailey may be pregnant!"

"That would be great!" replied Pamela warmly. She knew how much it meant to Arliss and Bob to have their laboratory animals reproduce.

"Joan tells me that the two of you are helping with Mr. Grant's murder investigation," offered Arliss, bracing herself by grasping Pamela's desk as she scooted her bottom around trying to find a comfortable position in the seat of the desk chair.

"Yes," said Pamela, "Joan conned me into this—and now I'm thoroughly entrenched."

"Just as always," said Arliss. "You know you can't resist a good murder case, Pam." Arliss gave her the eye.

"I can't in this case, Arliss," replied Pamela, "because it appears the police may have arrested the wrong man." She nodded back to her friend.

"Leave it to you and Joan," muttered Arliss, shaking her head, "to determine when the police have made a mistake."

"Wait a minute, missy!" exclaimed Joan. "You don't know everything that's gone on recently! You've been all wrapped up in impending mommyhood and furry pets, so you haven't kept up to speed on the details of this case."

"This case!" Arliss cried. "Joan, you're beginning to sound like Pam. Now both of you are detectives!"

"No, we're not detectives," noted Joan, precisely, "we're scientists, and as scientists we have certain skills and methods that we can utilize to assist Mr. Grant in his time of need."

"I see," said Arliss, "so if Mr. Grant didn't kill his wife, who did?" She looked from one friend to another with a shrug.

"We're not quite certain yet," replied Joan sheepishly, "but Pamela's working on it."

"And your job—in this investigation, Joan—was to get Pam involved," explained Arliss. "Looks like you've done that." She twisted uncomfortably in the desk chair.

"Pamela is the one with the police experience after all," Joan observed as she leaned back and crossed her arms.

"Stop it, you two!" cried Pamela. "Listen, Arliss, Joan may have encouraged me to get involved, but once I spoke with James, I realized that something was amiss. I don't know if I can figure any of this puzzle out, but I'm going to do whatever I can to assist him. He's a fine young man in a horrible–tragic– situation. He's lost his wife and now everyone thinks he's responsible for her death. And, what's worse, he's given up."

"We're trying to get him to fight for himself," said Joan. "Imagine how you would feel, Arliss, if no one supported you and Bob when you two were working so hard to save the animal lab."

"It's true," agreed Arliss, glancing from one friend to another. "I'll never forget what you did for us then, Pam," she said with a sob. "Oh, no! Now I'm crying. I don't know why, but everything makes me cry nowadays. I started sobbing uncontrollably this morning when I dropped an egg on the floor while I was making breakfast."

"It's hormones, honey!" noted Joan. "They're running rampant through your system."

Arliss continued sobbing. Pamela rose from the sofa and grabbed several tissues from a box on the desk and handed them to Arliss.

"Here," she said to her friend. "Don't worry. It's normal."

Arliss patted the tears from her cheeks and gave Pamela a shy smile. Joan rolled her eyes. Pamela returned to her sofa with a snide look in Joan's direction.

"Anyway, Pamela," said Joan, changing the subject, "have you been making any progress on your examination of those recordings?"

"What recordings?" asked Arliss, dabbing the bundle of tissue against her dark eyes.

"Willard and I have been comparing the recording of James's wife's 911 call with previous recordings that were made of her as Assistant District Attorney," replied Pamela.

"Why?" asked Arliss, with a pout.

"At first, we thought the 911 call might be fake, but it isn't. I mean, it really is Stacy Grant."

"You're sure?" asked Joan.

"Quite," replied Pamela. "Willard and I ran the acoustic profiles together. That's definitely Stacy Grant's voice on the 911 call."

"So that means she made the call," said Joan, frowning and nodding.

"She must have," responded Arliss. Pamela looked from one friend to the other and listened to their comments. Then suddenly, she set down her thermos on the end table next to her sofa and stood up.

"Stay here," she said as she headed out the door. "I'll be back."

Chapter Twenty-Four

Luckily, Willard Swinton was in his office. It was early afternoon and he had apparently finished his lunch (which he often ate at his desk). Willard's handicap prevented him from doing too much walking, so going off-campus (or even on-campus) for a meal would be a major undertaking. At the moment, Willard was apparently grading papers. His head was down, focused on a paper in his lap, and his ever-present, ivory-handled cane was hanging over the back of his desk chair.

"Willard," she said breathlessly, as she ran into his office, "I'm so glad you're here. Are you too busy to talk to me now?" She moved inside and quickly closed his office door shut.

"Oh, intrigue, my dear!" exclaimed Willard, looking up from his paper, "do we have a break-through in our murder investigation?"

"Maybe," she replied. "Can we look at the acoustic output of those recordings of Stacy Grant's voice together?"

"Of course, my dear," he replied, setting his grading aside and reaching into a desk drawer and bringing out a compact disk."

Pamela pulled a chair from in front of Willard's desk to beside his desk chair and sat down. Willard inserted the disk into his hard drive and used his mouse to bring up his acoustic software program on his monitor. Pamela and Willard bent their heads toward the screen intently as they observed the line where they knew the acoustic output would appear as Willard pressed the "play" button. The sound of Stacy Grant's voice burst from the speakers embedded in the computer monitor.

"My husband . . . outside . . . trying to break in . . . please help!" This short call for help she had come to know so well. Probably, the entire town of Reardon had come to know it as well because it had been played and re-played many times over by the local media.

"Willard," she commenced, as they listened to the recording of Stacy Grant's voice again and again. "We agree that the voice we hear is Stacy Grant. Correct?"

"Yes, my dear," said Willard. "We've checked and double checked the voice on this recording against the voice on the other recordings. I believe we can definitely conclude that the voices are the same."

"Yes," noted Pamela. "The voices are the same, Willard. But that's the problem with our assumption."

"What?" he asked.

"We are assuming that just because the voice on the 911 recording is that of Stacy Grant, that means that Stacy Grant made that call to 911."

"What are you getting at, my dear?" asked Willard, his face childlike in eager anticipation.

"Could it be possible that the voice on the 911 recording is Stacy, but that she didn't make the call?"

"I don't see how . . . ." replied Willard, seeming befuddled as he appeared to work through the possibilities.

"I'm speculating here, so please go with me," she said to him, running a hand through her hair, her frustration evident.

"I'm with you, my dear," he agreed, "wherever you go. You say it's her voice, but she didn't make the call. Are you suggesting she was coerced?"

"No," said Pamela. "I don't think so, because I think that would register in her voice. Let's listen again. What are you hearing? I know you've been thinking there is something strange about it, right?"

They played the recording several more times, listening more carefully to minute changes in the pitch, intensity, and tempo of the speaking woman's vocal patterns.

"There is a strange quality to her vocal patterns," said Willard, "but I can't say it sounds like duress. Or at least, it doesn't sound like the duress that a person would experience if they were scared because someone was breaking into their home."

"I agree," said Pamela. "There's something else."

"Do you think she's afraid?" he asked. "Is that what you're hearing?"

They played the recording again.

"There's a disjointed quality to it," noted Pamela. "Listen."

"Yes," agreed Willard, a furrow forming between his eyes as he listened intently to the sound of Stacy Grant saying, "My husband . . . outside . . . trying to break in . . . please help!"

"It's disjointed," said Pamela again.

"But isn't that because she's scared?" asked Willard. "Fear will make people speak faster and in a more clipped fashion.

"It's different," argued Pamela. "It doesn't sound like fear."

"You don't think she sounds afraid?" asked Willard.

"No," said Pamela, looking directly at her colleague, her mouth dropping open suddenly. "Actually, she doesn't sound at all afraid. Now that I think about it. Her voice sounds quite calm. Look here at the frequency level—it's quite low for someone with her pitch range. If she were scared, her pitch level should be much higher. But it's actually remarkably low."

"My dear, you're right!" he exclaimed. "I think that may be the reason I've been thinking it sounded so unusual. Because, except for the disjointed, broken phrasing, she sounds remarkably calm for someone calling 911."

"And listen to her say, 'please help,'" said Pamela. "It sounds like she's saying 'Please help yourself to some more potatoes.'"

"Yes!" agreed Willard. "Surely, if you feared for your life so much that you were forced to call 911, you'd be more excited sounding than this woman. She sounds much more the way she sounds giving one of her courtroom speeches speeches."

"That's it!" cried Pamela. "Willard, you've got it!"

"What?" he asked.

"She sounds exactly like she does in her courtroom speeches," said Pamela. "I know what we have to do next."

"What, my dear?" he queried, his eyes wide with delight.

"We need to go through every single courtroom recording we have—or can find—of Stacy Grant and search for these exact phrases that appear in her 911 call."

"Oh, my, yes!" he said. "I see where you're going. But can we get any more audio of Stacy Grant speaking? The small sample we have doesn't include the phrases we need."

"I don't know. I believe Ginger Cooper indicated that WRER had quite a bit of b-roll footage of Stacy. All I originally asked for was enough so we could verify that the voice on the 911 recording was her."

"And it is," he agreed.

"I'll just have to contact Ginger and see if we can get more b-roll of Stacy."

"With Mrs. Grant working for the prosecutor's office, my dear, the television station is liable to have quite a bit of footage of her speaking—to juries, to the press—who knows what."

"I know," said Pamela, her enthusiasm plummeting. "This could prove to be a massively time-consuming project."

"But, looking on the bright side," he noted, "it's labor intensive and something the entire team can help with. Once we have the audio recordings and some recorders, we can all sit over at headquarters with headphones and each listen to different recordings until we come up with Stacy saying these exact four phrases."

"Do you think Martin will go for that?" she asked.

"Of course, my dear. Martin is a dear friend. He'll do anything to help James."

"Then so can we," she confirmed, holding out her hand which Willard took. The two shook grimly.

"What if we can't find these phrases?" he asked. "I mean, what if Stacy Grant never used any of these phrases in her courtroom speeches—or at least those speeches that were recorded for posterity?"

"Oh, I think we'll find them," said Pamela confidently. "I think we'll find them, because I think Stacy Grant's murderer found them."

"Oh," replied Willard, his entire body responding to her words with a quiver.

Joan appeared at Willard's door, breathless.

"Pamela, come quickly! Arliss's water just broke!"

Chapter Twenty-Five

The two professors ran back to Pamela's office, the sound of their heels clicking rapidly on the linoleum floor. Once inside her office, Pamela immediately saw the petrified Arliss standing beside her desk chair, clutching her belly, a puddle beneath her feet.

"It just happened, Pam," she moaned. "I'm sorry!"

"Oh, for heaven's sake, Arliss!" said Pamela, quickly moving to her friend. "There's nothing to be sorry about. Sit down." She forced Arliss back into the desk chair. "Did you call your OB?"

"No!" replied the pregnant woman, whining. "I didn't even think about him!"

"Why should she?" added Joan, on the other side of the chair. "After all, he's a man! What good are they?"

"Call him," Pamela ordered Arliss, lifting the receiver from her desk phone and handing it to Arliss. Arliss complied and a brief conversation between Arliss and what appeared to be her OB's secretary, indicated that Arliss would soon be on her way to the hospital.

"I'm supposed to go straight to the hospital. I can't even go home to get my bag," cried Arliss as she hung up. "I have all my things ready to go at home!" she wailed.

"Where's Bob?" asked Pamela, gathering her purse and keys.

"In class," said Arliss.

"We should wait for him to get out of class," said Joan.

"No time," replied Pamela, now helping Arliss to stand up.

"I'll go get him," said Joan as she turned to the door.

"He's not on campus!" cried Arliss. "He took his intro class on a field trip."

"Forget Bob!" ordered Pamela. "You help me get Arliss in my car and to the hospital."

She escorted Arliss, who was very wobbly now, out her office door and down the hallway. Willard was standing in his doorway watching them depart.

"Good luck, Arliss!" he called to the mother-to-be. "I'll call Martin about those recordings, Pamela!"

"Thanks, Willard," Pamela yelled back at him as she and Joan helped Arliss through the stairwell doors and down the stairs to the main floor. Once there, they carefully guided her out the side entrance to Blake Hall and into the parking lot. Luckily, Pamela had parked her Civic near the side entrance. First, because she had a two-door, she had Joan climb into the back seat. Then, she helped Arliss into the front passenger seat and carefully buckled her in.

"Joan, while I'm driving, you call Jane Marie and have her have Bob meet us at the hospital as soon as he returns from the field trip. Oh, which hospital, Arliss?"

"Reardon General," replied Arliss with a death grip on her stomach. "The emergency room entrance they said."

"Did you get that, Joan?" asked Pamela.

"I got it. Good lord, Pamela," sneered Joan, "look at the mess in your back seat. Do you ever clean back here?"

"Would you rather stay here, Joan?" snipped Pamela, with a quick turn of her head.

"No, no! Just get going!" Pamela pulled out of the parking lot and sped as quickly as the posted limit would allow. Luckily, Reardon General was a main hospital and near campus.

"Call Jane Marie, Joan!" yelled Pamela. Joan pulled out her cell phone from a side compartment of her purse and tapped in several numbers. She was soon embroiled in conversation with Jane Marie who, Pamela gathered, from hearing Joan's end of the conversation, would see to it that

Bob Goodman would get to the hospital the minute he returned to campus.

"Oh, no!" yelled Arliss, a look of terror on her face, grabbing Pamela's shoulder, almost causing Pamela to ram into a streetlight on the roadside. Arliss squeezed her like she was kneading bread.

"What?" asked Pamela cringing.

"A cramp!" replied Arliss.

"Right!" noted Pamela, "it's called labor. Hang in there, sweetie."

"It hurts!" moaned Arliss.

"That's the result of hanky-panky, Missy . . . ." said Joan, leaning over and speaking into Arliss's ear.

"Joan!" cried Pamela. "Enough!" Joan leaned back into the car seat.

It was a short drive and they arrived in minutes even though it seemed like hours. Pamela pulled into the emergency entrance and stopped. She extracted Arliss from the front seat. Then, Joan walked Arliss into the hospital while Pamela quickly found a parking space and then joined them. As she entered the hospital, she could see a nurse leading Joan and Arliss, now seated in a wheel chair, through a set of double doors. She quickly caught up to them.

"Mrs. Goodman," the nurse said. "Doctor Doolittle called to tell us that you were on the way. We're all ready for you." She smiled down at Arliss, who chose that moment to have another contraction.

"Dr. Doolittle?" Joan asked Pamela as they walked behind. "A great name for an OB, right?"

"And for two animal lovers. Probably means he's very hands-off," offered Pamela with a grin.

"So he won't give her any drugs?" asked Joan.

"Who knows?" replied Pamela.

"Maybe he won't even show up," suggested Joan.

"Whatever he does," noted Pamela, "he's sure to send a huge bill." They laughed together with a mixture of joy, excitement, and trepidation.

The nurse led the trio through a maze of windowless hallways, pushing Arliss in the wheelchair while Joan and Pamela followed behind. Eventually, after a long trip on an elevator, they arrived at what was apparently the maternity ward. The nurse rolled the wheelchair into an empty patient room.

"Ladies," she said to Joan and Pamela, "you'll have to wait outside for a while. But you'll be able to come back in as soon as your friend is settled."

"Wonderful," said Pamela.

"Great," added Joan.

"Has the husband been informed?" asked the nurse.

"Yes," replied Pamela. "He teaches at Grace and he's on a field trip now. We left a message for him to get here as soon as he returns."

"Good," said the nurse and she hurried into Arliss's room, shutting the door as she entered.

"Maybe while we're waiting, you'll want to go down and clean out your car," suggested Joan.

"Joan!" cried Pamela, aghast. "My back seat isn't that dirty!"

"I didn't mean your back seat," whispered Joan. "I meant the front seat—where Arliss was sitting. It's not pretty. She soaked through on your seat."

"Don't worry about it," replied Pamela. "There are worse things. We're going to stay here and support Arliss. My car upholstery is the least of my worries."

With that, the sound of Arliss wailing in pain broke the relative quiet of the hallway.

"Are you sure?" asked Joan with a sly glare.

After a few minutes, the nurse who had guided them to the maternity ward reappeared and motioned them to enter Arliss's room. The two women cautiously stepped forward and walked into the small patient room that was outfitted with monitors and devices for measuring the progress of labor and the well-being of the unborn baby. Arliss was now lying in the only bed in the room, wearing one of those blue and white patterned hospital gowns that never flattered anyone. She looked miserable. Various wires attached her stomach to the monitoring equipment.

"Is Bob here yet?" Arliss asked.

"No," said Pamela, "but he'll be here soon. Jane Marie will get him here as soon as he gets back."

"She'll see to it he gets here fast, Arliss," replied Joan, encouragingly. "Don't worry."

Arliss smiled broadly, but her eyes belied her true feelings. Joan and Pamela beamed back, but Arliss's face slowly turned to an excruciating grimace as another contraction racked her body. The nurse rushed over to the monitor and began reading the printouts.

"Here comes a big one," observed the nurse as she looked at the paper. "Now, just breathe slowly. Don't hold your breath," she commanded gently. Arliss looked like she was attempting to follow the directions but as the contraction peaked, she clenched her teeth and appeared to be holding her breath. When the contraction subsided, she fell back on the bed, gulping for air.

"You need to breathe during the contractions," noted the nurse as she re-engaged the electrical nodes that had apparently been pulled off during Arliss's contraction. "My, these are strong ones. You're moving right along quickly, Mrs. Goodman. The doctor will be in shortly to see how far you're dilated."

"Where's Bob?" repeated Arliss, breathless and flushed, sweat forming on her forehead.

"You ladies can help to keep her calm, until the husband arrives," suggested the nurse as she exited the room.

Pamela and Joan moved closer to the bed—one of them on either side. The medical paraphernalia that surrounded their friend made her look like the victim of some alien abduction. With her protruding belly, Pamela couldn't help but imagine Arliss lying inside a spaceship waiting the delivery of some combination alien-earthling child. Of course, that daydream wasn't far off the mark, given Arliss's passion for animals.

"Does it hurt?" asked Joan.

"Not now," replied Arliss weakly.

"When it starts up again," suggested Joan, "you can squeeze our hands." She took Arliss's right hand and Pamela took her left. Arliss looked up at her friends and gave a tiny smile. She squeezed each hand warmly. Pamela looked at Joan and thought that for all of her bravado and wise-ass comments, when the chips were down, Joan was there. She was glad that she and Joan could be here for Arliss because the three of them had been friends for years, and Joan and Arliss had supported her and her crime-detecting efforts over the years—even when they thought she was crazy–which was more often than not.

They were—all three of them—a team, and when one needed advice or assistance, the other two came to the rescue. Needless to say, maybe because she was the youngest and had the most to learn, Arliss was often the most in need. Pamela remembered how she and Joan had assisted Arliss in her volatile romance with Bob Goodman, their wedding that almost never happened, and now the birth of their first child. She almost thought of Arliss as her sister, which was hard to do because Pamela was an only child. Even so, Arliss and Joan were both very dear to her, and now as she held her honorary sister's hand along with her other honorary sister Joan, as they awaited the birth of what felt like a niece or nephew, she looked down at Arliss's face and noted the stream of tears dripping from her eyes. Maybe they were tears of pain, but maybe they were tears of joy. Pamela reached up to her face with her free hand and felt the tears in her own eyes. These were tears of joy. No doubt about it.

"Arliss! Honey!" called out Bob Goodman, rushing into the room. "I came as soon as I could!" He ran to the bed and embraced his wife. Pamela and Joan edged back and out of the room, allowing the couple to be alone.

"It's good he arrived in time," said Joan. Pamela looked at her friend, who turned her head away. Joan couldn't fool her. She saw the tears in Joan's eyes too.

Chapter Twenty-Six

They had sat in the maternity ward waiting room for hours. Pamela could have sworn when they brought Arliss in that little Goodwin would be popping out in no time at all. She was mistaken. As the hours rolled by, Joan and Pamela utilized the time to mull over the James Grant murder case. Pamela revealed to Joan what she and Willard suspected about the 911 recording. As it got to be suppertime, Pamela gathered her courage and phoned her husband.

"Rocky, honey," she began, "I'm probably not going to make it home for dinner tonight." She readied herself for his negative response.

"You're not down at that jail again, are you?" he queried. "Another political strategy meeting?"

"No, dear," she assured her mate. "I'm at the hospital . . . ."

"Hospital!" he cried, "What's wrong?"

"Oh, Rocky," she said, chuckling, "nothing's wrong with me, dear. Arliss is in labor. Joan and I brought her down here. Bob is here now and Joan and I are waiting."

"Do you know how much longer it will be?" he asked, assuaged, his voice expressing his relief.

"No," she sighed. "I really thought she'd have it by now! I mean her water broke and that's often a sign that things will go fast. But it's her first so they're usually slower. I just don't know, but Joan and I are prepared to stay however long it takes, if you don't mind."

"I don't mind, but maybe I should come down there. I don't like the idea of you driving home after dark, considering the problems you've been having lately." *If he only knew*, thought Pamela.

"I'll be fine," she assured Rocky. "I'll come right home as soon as the baby is born. I'll call you when I leave the hospital. It's Reardon General and I just have to drive straight down Jackson–no side streets."

"Okay," he agreed, "but call when you leave."

Okay, bye." She hung up. Joan gave her one of her feminist leers that she liked to do whenever she thought Pamela was acting too "wifey" as she called it.

"So, is he rushing right down here to save you?" she sneered.

"No," said Pamela with a glare, "he trusts me."

"A likely story," huffed Joan. "That man would have you dipped in bronze and set you on the mantelpiece if he had his way."

"I may have forgotten to mention to you that the police were at our door in the middle of the night a few days back because there was some unmarked vehicle staking out our house."

"Oh, really?" she replied.

"Yes," said Pamela, "Shoop is having me followed now ever since I got that threatening phone call."

"They still don't know who it was who called?"

"They don't," said Pamela, "but I think I do."

"Who?" asked Joan, smiling and rubbing her hands together like some Hollywood gossip hound.

"Victor Baines."

"The same guy who roughed you up after the meeting?" asked Joan, skeptically.

"Yeah," said Pamela. "I haven't told Rocky about that either, so if he asks, don't let on."

"My lips are sealed," Joan replied, giving her the key turning at the mouth gesture. "You know, that Baines guy didn't exactly seem like the type to threaten anyone. He's too–uh, fat."

"Right, and according to Mrs. Brewster, he's still recovering from by-pass surgery."

"How did you talk to her?" asked Joan.

"She came to see me after class."

"The mayor's wife? Why?"

"She wanted to plead with me to stay out of the investigation," said Pamela with a chuckle.

"Wow!" whispered Joan, the hospital setting muting what would otherwise be a much larger reaction. "Doesn't that tell you something?"

"I thought it did," said Pamela, "but after talking to the woman, I get the distinct impression that she's clueless about the inner workings of her husband's campaign. She just heard I was somehow involved with James's investigation and she'd heard about my involvement with previous cases, and so she just assumed I might damage her husband's campaign."

"It could all be an act," suggested Joan. "Many very smart people are capable of playing dumb when it suits their purposes."

"Are you speaking of anyone in particular?" asked Pamela. Joan's knowing expression mystified her.

"No, just something Conrad said," said Joan with a smile.

"Conrad?" exclaimed Pamela. "You mean, Martin's sleazy investigator? That Gates guy?"

"What do you mean 'sleazy'?" Joan huffed, her jaw decidedly dropped.

"Oh, come on, Joan," said Pamela, "the man had a ton of Vitalis in his hair and a suit jacket at least two sizes two small."

"Surface features," said Joan, "totally on the surface. The man is a fascinating mélange of amazing experiences. You wouldn't believe the places he's been and some of the things he's done. I probably couldn't tell you, because of your sensitive nature . . . ."

"My sensitive nature!" cried Pamela, "Joan Bentley! You're smitten! With a gumshoe!"

"He's completely different from your average academic," continued Joan, "who are mostly totally predictable. Now, Conrad, on the other hand, never ceases to surprise me."

"Surprise you?" exclaimed Pamela. "You sound as if you've already been out . . . . Joan, have you gone out with that man?"

"So what if I have?" chirped Joan, sweetly, smiling benignly at Pamela over her shoulder.

"You barely met him!" shrieked Pamela in a stage whisper.

"Who are you, my mother?" responded Joan. "I'm of age. I don't need your approval to date."

"But, Joan!" continued Pamela. "The man is so far beneath your usual . . . choices. I mean, you typically have much better . . . taste."

"Oh my, aren't we superior!" scowled Joan. "You think you're better than anyone else because you married an Army cook!"

"That's not the point!" she shot back.

"What is the point?" asked Joan, now nose to Pamela's nose.

"Oh, for heaven's sake," said Pamela, leaning back in the hospital chair. She looked around and was gratified that there were no other people in the maternity ward waiting room at the moment. The last thing she should be doing is fighting with Joan while they sat here and waited for Arliss's baby to be born.

"How long have we been here?" asked Joan, changing the subject, much to Pamela's relief.

"At least six hours," replied Pamela, looking down at her watch.

"Do you want to wait here while I go down to the hospital cafeteria and get us some sandwiches?" Joan asked.

Pamela's stomach lurched at the thought of sandwiches made by anyone except her sandwich king Rocky. Eating a regular sandwich was like eating raw cardboard, she guessed.

At that moment, Bob came out of Arliss's room. Pamela realized that the agonizing cries that had been coming from the room over the last few hours (and that she had been trying to ignore unsuccessfully) had slowed and ultimately ceased. Bob looked around quickly and then noticed Joan and Pamela sitting alone in the small waiting room. He hurried over to the two women.

"It's a boy!" he beamed.

"Oh, Bob!" exclaimed Pamela. "We're so happy for you and Arliss!" She flung her arms around Bob's neck and squeezed him tight.

"Wonderful!" added Joan as she gave Bob a small hug.

"Here," said Bob, reaching into his shirt pocket and pulling out two blue cellophane-wrapped cigars. "They're bubble gum." He handed one to Pamela and one to Joan.

"How is Arliss?" asked Pamela, tucking the cigar in her purse.

"Tired but happy," he replied. "Oh, and the baby weighs seven pounds, fifteen ounces. We're going to call him Noah."

"Very appropriate," noted Joan, unwrapping her gum cigar and taking a bite.

"Ideal," added Pamela. "I'm sure he'll turn out to be an animal lover just like his parents." She beamed at Bob and they hugged again.

"I'm going to go back in. The doctor says you two may come in for just a few minutes."

"Wonderful," replied Pamela. "Is that okay with Arliss?"

"She wants you to come in. She knows you've both been here the whole time."

Bob led the way into the small room. Arliss looked much calmer than she had when they brought her in. She was sitting up in bed, her black kinky curls drenched and plastered to her head. In her arms she held a tiny bundle in a blue blanket.

"Oh, Arliss, he's beautiful!" whispered Pamela as she bent down to get a better view of the small pink face with his eyes closed. Joan followed and stood beside Pamela, squinting at the tiny face.

"Look at you," Joan said, chewing her cigar gum, "your mother surely gave us a merry chase today! We thought we'd have to deliver you ourselves on Aunt Pamela's office floor!"

"If you had," replied Arliss, beaming, "I know you would have done a wonderful job!"

"Arliss is right," said Bob coming up behind the two women and putting his arms around their shoulders. "We can't thank you enough for helping her out. Who would have thought that Noah would pick right during my mass lecture class to make his entrance? He obviously has two very good aunts."

"We were glad to help," said Pamela.

"Two very hungry aunts," added Joan. "I think we're going to let you and your baby get some rest, Arliss. Pamela and I need to get going and get some supper."

"Oh, absolutely!" replied Arliss. "Thank you, again, you two! I'll never forget how you helped me today!" Each new aunt gave one last glance at their new nephew and then headed out of Arliss's room. Bob followed and said farewell to them outside of her door.

"It's after six," noted Joan as they headed through the hospital's main lobby.

"Right," said Pamela. "I'm going home. Rocky will probably warm up something for me. Shall I drop you off on campus so you can get your car or do you just want me to take you straight to your apartment?"

"Umm," said Joan thoughtfully, "you can go on without me."

"What?" asked Pamela. "How are you going to get home?"

"Um," Joan hesitated, looking around, then turned to her friend and whispered, "Conrad will take me home."

Pamela looked up to see the seedy investigator leaning against a pillar near the entrance to Reardon General, a stereotypical toothpick in his teeth. He grinned as he saw Joan walking towards him.

Chapter Twenty-Seven

She had arrived home after seven that night and had collapsed in bed after a quick supper. Rocky, bless his heart, had not hounded her about her day—evidently helping a pregnant friend give birth was an acceptable reason for being hours late. She had slept soundly and awakened refreshed. Amazingly enough, she felt a new insight into how to proceed with her investigation of the 911 recording.

At work, she immediately sought out Willard. As he had not yet arrived, she went to her office. After settling in, she called Ginger Cooper at WRER. The reporter was in early today and anxious to hear how Pamela's sleuthing was coming along.

"Dr. Barnes," said Ginger, "have you found anything from those voice samples we sent you?"

"Miss Cooper," responded Pamela, "I'll tell you that they're proving very helpful. Unfortunately, we're finding that we now have an even bigger mystery on our hands. It appears that we're going to need a much larger sample than just the few seconds you sent us."

"Bummer," retorted Ginger Cooper. "That's a problem. My assistant sent you the only recording we have catalogued just for Stacy Grant. I'm sure we have additional footage of her on b-roll in our archives, but it's probably catalogued differently–maybe under the various court cases she worked on, maybe under the DA's name, or any number of other possibilities. It would take quite a bit of manpower and lots of time to track down every audio segment we might have for Stacy Grant. If it were just up to me, Dr. Barnes, I'd do it in a heartbeat, but I don't think the station manager would sanction the time and personnel involved in such a task."

"I understand," replied Pamela. "I'm just wondering if there's any way we—I mean—I could get access to your archives and search for Stacy's audio myself."

"I don't know," said Cooper. "I could talk to the station manager. We usually don't have non-station personnel working in the editing suite. You'd have to use the editing suite to go through all that b-roll and we only have three units. If you tied up one of our units for a long time, it would make our work pretty difficult."

"I see that," noted Pamela. "There's no way we could get a hold of the b-roll for these various court cases or the prosecutor's office and go through them on our own?"

"Afraid not," replied the reporter, "as our videotape is designed to run only on our special machines. It's not like you can play it on your home DVR. I mean, I can certainly keep looking for more segments of her voice, but I can't guarantee when I'll be able to track any of it down."

"Ginger," said Pamela, after a pause, "how would someone get access to any of this b-roll? I mean, I'm contacting you directly. What if someone else wanted to use some of your footage? Is there a method for obtaining it? Do you ever loan it out? Or is what I'm doing—by asking to see it—unusual?"

"No, not really," replied Ginger Cooper, "sometimes we loan out footage to individuals to make local commercials or as legal evidence—or any number of other reasons. But usually, the person who needs it knows pretty much what they want. Or they know how to find it. There are a number of people in town who are proficient with our type of editing suites."

"What about that recent Brewster ad?" she queried. "The slick one with the cartoon characters that makes Brewster look like a super hero? Seems there was quite a bit of footage of Brewster in that."

"Yeah," replied the WRER anchor, "that was certainly one of the better local spots I've ever seen. The Brewster campaign is definitely getting more sophisticated in their PR."

"Do you know anyone in their campaign?" Pamela asked.

"No," said Ginger, "I pretty much try to keep out of both campaigns personally. You know, to remain unbiased. Believe me; it's hard to do, what with Brewster running this town into the ground for . . . . please don't get me going."

"I'm sorry," replied Pamela. "I'm not trying to cause you any trouble. I'm just trying to figure out where to go from here. We really need more footage of Stacy Grant speaking. We need a large sample and we need it quickly."

"You might check the DA's office," suggested Ginger. "I mean, Stacy is—was— one of theirs. Maybe they kept video or audio records of her court cases."

"I'll certainly try that," agreed Pamela. "Anyway, thank you, Miss Cooper . . . Ginger. You've been more than helpful."

"You're welcome, Dr. Barnes. Good luck." With that, Pamela hung up. *The DA's office.* At Ginger Cooper's suggestion, she called the local office of the prosecuting attorney and explained her request. She was informed that the DA did not maintain any video or audio records of their assistants in court.

"Pamela." She heard Willard's voice as she looked up from her desk and saw her friend standing in her doorway leaning on his cane. His face gleamed with a broad smile.

"Oh, Willard," she sighed. "I've tried both WRER and the DA's office to try to get us additional footage of Stacy Grant, but no luck.

"Then my news will be most welcome, my dear," said Willard. "I believe I know where we can get exactly what we need."

"Where?" she asked.

"At WPUR," replied Willard.

"What?"

"Yes," said Willard, with a gleeful grin as he wobbled in to her office. "Martin informs me that our campaign—I mean, James's campaign—has produced several clever video ads which utilized footage that they got from some local television stations. Of course, none of this footage includes Stacy, but Martin contacted the person who did our ads and found out where she got the footage she needed."

"And?"

"The local access station."

"What?"

"Local access," repeated Willard. "It's WPUR. It's very shoestring, you know. Lots of Grace students evidently use it. Amateur shows and so forth. The Grace media department often produces programs on it. Anyway, WPUR maintains an extensive library of b-roll of all sorts of documentary-type footage. Martin spoke with them and we are more than welcome to come down there and go through their library of material. They actually are delighted to have us, particularly since you're involved."

"Then what are we waiting for?" she asked. "Can you contact Martin and set up a time for the whole team to meet down there? Maybe later today?"

"I'll call him right away," replied Willard, hobbling out of her office and down the hallway. He almost smashed head on into Joan who was entering just as he was exiting.

"Where's the fire?" called out Joan to Willard's rapidly departing figure. "I've never seen him move that fast," she remarked to Pamela as she wandered into the office and casually placed herself on her favorite chair.

"We may have a break in the case," said Pamela. "Can you meet with us this afternoon? Probably around four?"

"I can," said Joan, perking up, "but I was planning on going over to the hospital to visit Arliss and the baby."

"Maybe we can sneak out at lunch time for a quick peek," suggested Pamela, as she too wanted to get another view of the new baby.

"Won't do," replied Joan. "Have to go during visiting hours, two to five."

"Hmm," said Pamela with a sigh. "It's going to have to wait. If we find what we're after right away, maybe you and I can stop by the hospital after we leave WPUR."

"WPUR?" asked Joan. "Isn't that public access? What do we need to do there?"

"Listen to acres of b-roll footage for audio of Stacy Grant," replied Pamela.

"Ugh," responded Joan. "That sounds boring!"

"Conrad will be there," Pamela said with an inviting leer.

"Of course, then, I'll do my part for the cause," said Joan, lifting her chest proudly.

"I figured as much," said Pamela. "How did your date go last night?"

"Swimmingly," replied Joan, stretching out, arms behind her head. "He's such a fascinating man!" She placed one heeled foot neatly over the other.

"I hope you continue to believe that when you start to regale him with tales of your latest ed psych report and his eyes glaze over."

"I can make dry prose sound entertaining," said Joan with a gestural flourish.

"I don't doubt it," offered Pamela, "I certainly hope that Mr. Gates appreciates how lucky he is."

"I have talents, Pamela, of which you are unaware," whispered Joan conspiratorially.

"My ears, Joan!" cried Pamela, covering them with her hands in mock horror.

Willard popped back inside her office door.

"We're on for four this afternoon, ladies," he announced breathlessly. "WPUR, south on Highway 22 about six miles south of town."

"I know where it is, Willard," replied Pamela. "We'll be there."

"With our magnifying glasses in tow!" added Joan. They all laughed and Willard headed back to his office.

Chapter Twenty-Eight

At four o'clock that afternoon, Pamela drove up outside of public access television station WPUR, located out in the "boonies" just off the highway. With Joan in the front seat, the two professors pulled into the small gravel lot in front of the white clapboard building which sported a dilapidated set of four giant black call letters carved out of wood and each surrounded with what appeared to be blinking Christmas tree lights. A large number of cars were already gathered and Pamela could see Martin and Willard who had obviously come together surrounded by Conrad Gates and a group of young college students standing in front of the main entrance. The women got out of their vehicle and headed over to their group.

"Dr. Barnes, Dr. Bentley," said Martin Dobbs warmly, "as you can see, we're here in force. I hope we have a sufficient number of people to accomplish this task for you."

"You probably have more than enough," responded Pamela. "I don't know how many video editors this station has. We'll see."

"Shall we go in?" Dobbs asked and pointed the way for the group to enter the building.

Inside, Martin encountered a secretary seated at a desk immediately before them. He spoke quietly to the woman and she left through a door in the small wood-paneled lobby. Shortly after, she returned with a small man wearing a huge pair of horned-rimmed glasses and wearing a white, short-sleeved shirt. The man came immediately to Martin and greeted him and all of the adults in the entourage. Martin spoke with the man briefly and then the man led the entire group through the lobby door. They followed him through a maze of hallways past various small recording studios and editing stations. At the end of a long hallway, he led them into a large room outfitted with several tables. On one table were placed four large television monitors with additional equipment surrounding each of them. Pamela recognized these units as the editing bays. On the second table, piled up high were a dozen or so DVRs–each marked with a hand-written label.

"We've set this room up just for you, Dr. Barnes," the glasses-wearing man said to her, and then turning to Martin, he added "and Mr. Dobbs, you can assign four people to actually sit here at the monitors and look at the video. You may want to have your other folks, go through the stacks of DVRs my staff has pulled for you from our archives. We've pulled anything labeled 'Stacy Grant' or 'DA's office' or 'prosecutor' or anything similar to that. As you can tell, there are dozens of DVRs. I don't know exactly what you're looking for, so I really don't know how long it might take you to find it—if you can."

"Um, thank you, um . . ." Pamela began.

"Peter Simms," he said. "I'm the manager of WPUR. As a public access station, it's our duty to assist the . . . uh, public to obtain access to media. This is, admittedly, a strange request, but certainly within our mission."

"Thank you, Mr. Simms," she continued. "You've been extremely helpful." She shook his hand and the man left the group to their own devices. Immediately, Pamela looked around at the potential manpower available.

"How do you want to proceed, Pamela?" asked Martin Dobbs, his sparkling smile never more gleaming than today.

"I think we'll probably need to take turns at the editing bays," she suggested as she looked at the massive amount of material they would have to view. "Why don't we start out by taking hour-long shifts and see what we find. Who wants to view video and who wants to keep records?"

Several students raised their hands and Pamela stationed four at the monitors and seated the remainder at the other large table full of DVRs.

"Okay," she said to the group. "When you're looking at video on the monitor, you're looking specifically for the murdered assistant district attorney Stacy Grant. We need audio from her—but we need very specific words. It doesn't really matter if the words are together. If you find just one of the words, call me over to your station right away. I'll want to hear it and I'll want to make an audio recording of it myself. The words we need to hear Stacy saying are, 'My husband . . . outside . . . trying to . . . break in. Please help!' Do you have that?"

The group of students nodded, some jotted down the phrases, and then quietly went to work. Joan assumed the role of managing the group working at the table going through the DVRs—along with Conrad Gates. Willard and Martin stood behind the students listening to and watching the videos on the editing bay monitors. Pamela moved around the room, waiting to be called over when one of the viewing students located one of the phrases in Stacy's 911 call.

It didn't take long. Within fifteen minutes, one of the students waved his hand in excitement. Martin and Willard rushed to his side and the student raised the volume so the three adults could hear, and ran the recording back to a segment where Stacy Grant was speaking to a jury. Pamela moved behind the group and they all listened as the woman on the screen said, "I don't know what the defendant was trying to do, but I do know what he did." Pamela motioned for the student to run the short segment back and play it again. She listened again as Stacy Grant said the words 'trying to' in her jury speech. Reaching into her purse that she had set on a nearby console, she brought out a small tape recorder, and when the student played the segment a third time, she recorded the two important words.

Gratified that they had found one of the four phrases they were seeking, she hoped they would be able to find the remaining three phrases as quickly. Unfortunately, it took longer than she expected. After an hour, one of the girls located 'break in' from a section of one of Stacy's press conferences. On this recording, Stacy was responding to a question about how long she thought it would take for her to become accustomed to working for the DA, and she said it might take time to 'break her in.' Pamela took the phrase although she realized she'd have to dub out the 'her.' She wondered if the killer had done that or if the killer had found another section where Stacy had said 'break in' as a complete phrase.

They continued in this same manner and eventually they found the word 'outside.'

They had gone through all the DVRs related to Stacy's cases at the DA's office. They were now into other recordings for the DA's office—much more general stuff. Every once in a while, Stacy would appear in a segment, but the monitor people had to fast forward through a lot of material until they finally came to something featuring the murder victim actually speaking. After several hours and much frustration, one of the students at one of the monitors called out to them.

"I think I've got her saying 'husband'," he cried with excitement. Martin, Willard, and Pamela zipped behind him as he played the video at a higher volume for all to hear. Stacy Grant appeared on the screen. The DA stood to her side.

"What a great day for the DA's office," said the man on the screen that Pamela knew as Charles Findlay, "and especially for our young ADA Stacy Grant. Two convictions in one week, Stacy! That's some kind of record."

"I'm certainly thrilled," replied Stacy as the camera panned over the faces of her office mates out in the audience. "But it's not a personal victory—it's a victory for our entire office!"

There was applause from everyone present. Someone in the group pushed a man forward towards Stacy. It was James. He laughed and came forward and joined the DA and Stacy.

"And who is this young man, Stacy?" asked the DA, laughing.

"This is my husband, sir!" she responded. "He's gone without supper for weeks so I could get those convictions for you!" The audience laughed.

At that point, Pamela motioned for the student to stop the recording.

"Replay, just before she says 'husband' so I can record it," she asked him. The routine was repeated and eventually Pamela had all the phrases that comprised Stacy Grant's 911 call saved on her small audio recorder—all except the phrase 'please help.' She knew she could probably make her case to the police without this last phrase, but she believed this particular phrase would cement her argument because it was the most emotional. She pleaded with the group to continue to search for the final phrase. It was now after eight. Conrad and Martin had gone out several hours ago and had brought in take-out for the group. They were all tired but still motivated. Around midnight, a small female student with her eyes glued to her monitor, raised her hand.

"Dr. Barnes," she whispered, "I think I found 'please help.'"

Chapter Twenty-Nine

"Mrs. Brewster," said Pamela, greeting the mayor's wife warmly at the top of the steps of Hap Brewster's impressive campaign headquarters. Far grander than the James Grant campaign headquarters, this edifice was a two-story brick structure near the center of town and it looked like the site of major patriotic activity, complete with red, white, and blue bunting encasing the top of the white portico that covered the stairs spanning the entire front of the building. Large windows towered up from the first floor offices as high as the second story, each window sporting massive full-color posters of the incumbent himself complete with exhortations to "vote" for the man.

"Dr. Barnes," responded Katherine Brewster as she guided the professor into the inner sanctum of her husband's re-election headquarters. Pamela had called earlier and requested an opportunity to visit the Brewster campaign site and Katherine Brewster—possibly still feeling guilty for harassing her—had volunteered to show her around personally. The political wife escorted Pamela into a huge two-story lobby, complete with glittering chandelier. At the back of the lobby, a grand staircase circled up to the second floor. Several hallways led off of the lobby directly. A lone sentry stood guard at a beautiful mahogany desk directly beside the staircase.

"George," said Katherine to the old man behind the desk, "I'm going to be showing Dr. Barnes around the facility. Where is everyone today?"

"Don't rightly know, Mrs. Brewster," replied the wizened gentleman. Probably all up in the main office."

"No doubt having a meeting," said Katherine to Pamela, smiling. "Why don't we start down here?" She led Pamela down a side hallway and into a large room where numerous campaign volunteers were seated at tables. Most were manning phones. Some were working at tables in the center of the room, stuffing envelopes or folding flyers.

"This is where our volunteers work," said Katherine. "We have hundreds, many of them students, as you can see."

"Yes," said Pamela, "it's wonderful when students become involved in the political process."

"I agree, Dr. Barnes," replied Katherine Brewster, beaming. "You and I are certainly not as different as I first thought."

"No," agreed Pamela. "There are many things that we have in common. I'm curious, Mrs. Brewster. . . ."

"Katherine."

"Katherine, I'm curious about those very clever ads your husband's campaign has been running lately."

"Oh, you mean the ones with the little cartoon characters?" she squealed, delighted.

"Yes, they portray Mayor Brewster as a sort of super hero."

"I know. They created that ad right here in-house," she said, the definite increase in her pitch level indicating her enthusiasm.

"Really? It was very sophisticated," Pamela gushed appropriately.

"Let's go over to our communications suite," suggested Katherine. "I'll show you the amazing equipment they use to make those ads."

"Wonderful!" cried Pamela. "It's hard to believe that anyone could create something so clever right here in Reardon."

"Oh, yes," noted Katherine. "We have a group of very talented artists and communication specialists."

"I can see that you do," said Pamela smiling, as she followed Katherine back to the lobby and down another side hallway on the opposite side. The two women followed the narrow pathway around until they finally reached a sealed and padded door at the end of the hall. A glass window in the door revealed a massive electronic control center—far more communication and video/audio editing equipment than Pamela had seen at WPUR. Katherine peeked into the window. As no one apparently was inside, she carefully opened the door and gestured for Pamela to enter.

Pamela wandered wide-eyed into the room, its walls totally encrusted with equipment from floor to ceiling. On the far wall, a built-in counter jutted out. On it, a master control console oversaw a group of eight television screens on the wall above. Katherine Brewster gestured for Pamela to feel free to look around. Pamela moved over to the counter and sat at one of the sliding/rolling chairs. She examined the equipment on the counter, noting particularly the audio capabilities of the unit as indicated by the various markings on the dials and levers in front of her.

"You must have a lot of people working on your commercials," Pamela said.

"Oh, I don't really know," laughed Katherine. "Harold doesn't really discuss the technicalities of it all with me, but I do know that it's very elaborate."

"I can see that it is," agreed Pamela.

Three men entered the room. The first was Hap Brewster. He was followed by his two cronies—Victor Baines and Kevin Sturges.

"Darling," Brewster called out to his wife. "What brings you down here to the basement?"

"Harold calls anything technical 'the basement,'" whispered Katherine. "Harold, this is Dr. Pamela Barnes from Grace's Psychology Department. Mitchell Marks asked me to show her around."

Pamela realized that Katherine was lying because she herself had asked for the tour. Even so, Katherine lied effortlessly and her fib only managed to provide an excuse for their presence in a place where they probably shouldn't be.

"Dr. Barnes," said Hap Brewster to Pamela, with a short, polite bow. The two men behind Brewster remained quiet. Victor Baines gave Pamela a slightly threatening stare. "We're happy to have you visiting our headquarters."

"Thank you, Mayor," responded Pamela. "Actually, I'm delighted to find you here—particularly with Mr. Baines— who I met the other day.   There's something I'd like to discuss with you."

"Really?" asked the mayor, looking quizzically from his wife to his two aides.

"Yes," Pamela continued. "Ever since I saw that commercial for your campaign—you know the one with you as a super hero and all the cartoon character villains–I was curious just how such an amazing piece of art could be constructed. I wondered if, perchance, you hired a specialist from outside–maybe New York or Los Angeles—to create it. It was so clever, it was just hard to believe that someone right here in Reardon actually made it."

"I'm happy to tell you, Dr. Barnes," said Brewster, puffing up, hands on his lapels, "that that ad was totally home grown. We had a number of our people working on it, didn't we, Kevin?" he asked the younger man behind him.

"Yes, sir," replied Kevin Sturges, hands in pockets. "Several of us worked late hours on that one, Boss!"

"You see, Dr. Barnes," said Brewster, "we don't need to ship out anything to some high falutin' New York or Los Angeles firm. We can do all that fancy pro-duction stuff right here at home!" He rocked back and forth on his heels, arms folded.

"I see, Mayor, that you truly do have the technical facilities to accomplish practically anything your campaign needs done," she said pointedly looking from Brewster to Baines to Sturges.

"Just as I said," agreed the mayor, smiling.

"Of course," continued Pamela cautiously, "you surely wouldn't sanction your amazing technical suite here being used to manufacture false evidence?"

Brewster laughed and looked around at his wife and his men.

"What are you gettin' at, lady?" he asked, annoyed.

"I'm suggesting," she said, "that you—or one of your assistants—created the 911 tape that Stacy Grant supposedly sent to authorities out of segments of previous speeches she had given. You used the equipment here to splice those segments together so they sounded like a desperate woman who felt her husband was trying to kill her and was calling for help."

"What are you talking about?" Brewster shouted.

"Just this," she said, pulling her small tape recorder from her purse. She pressed the 'play' button and the 911 call from Stacy Grant filled the tech room. "My husband . . . outside . . . trying to . . . break in. Please help!"

"Look, Dr. . . uh. . . Barnes," continued Brewster, "I don't know what you're gettin' at. That sure sounds like that call from Grant's wife to 911. What makes you think it was made here?"

"I don't know for sure that it . . . ."

"Oh, you're just guessing," interrupted Brewster.

"Harold," cautioned Katherine, "your blood pressure!" She grabbed his arm in an attempt to calm him.

"What I do know, Mayor Brewster," continued Pamela, "is that I—we—have proof that the 911 call from Stacy Grant was doctored."

"Doctored? How?" asked Victor Baines. He looked sick and redder than he had when he banged on her car door. Kevin Sturges grabbed Baines's arm and attempted to hold him up.

"That 911 tape was composed of phrases from speeches Stacy Grant had given in her capacity as an assistant DA. She was either speaking to a jury or the press or in several other situations. We tracked down these audio recordings at WPUR and compared them acoustically. They match perfectly. And I don't just mean that the 911 tape is just Stacy's voice. I mean the phrases on the 911 tape are identical to those phrases. That is, someone spliced the phrases from these previous audio recordings of Stacy Grant and edited them together to make a fake 911 call that they then sent, which caused the police to come to the Grant home where they found Stacy dead."

"I don't get it," muttered Brewster. "Why would anyone do that? Besides, as long as the police got there when they did and arrested the killer, isn't that what counts?"

"If they actually arrested the real killer," said Pamela pointedly. "But, think about it, Mayor. Why would anyone go to all the trouble of faking a 911 call? Especially when the person who supposedly makes that call ends up dead? The obvious reason is to divert attention from the real killer. And who does this particular fake 911 call implicate? James Grant. Here's what I think happened. The real killer kills Stacy Grant, sends the fake 911 call and then leaves, just before James arrives, and just before the police arrive."

"But, Dr. Barnes," interjected Katherine, "that doesn't make any sense. How would this killer—even if this killer made this elaborate fake 911 call–how would this killer know that James Grant would show up and be kneeling over his wife's body right before the police arrived? It all seems ridiculous."

"I agree," said Pamela, "if it were just luck that James arrived when he did. But what if our clever killer not only made a fake 911 call, but also made a fake call from Stacy to her husband asking him to come home right away because she was scared. According to James and the phone company's records, that is exactly what happened. James claims that Stacy called him at the rally and urged him to rush home— which he did. James says that he had just found his wife's body and was trying to resuscitate her when the police arrived. James tells us that the call he got from Stacy was very short and disjointed—just like the fake 911 call."

"It sounds fascinating, Dr. Barnes," said Brewster, "but really a bit far-fetched. Don't you think, guys?"

"Definitely, Hap," agreed Baines.

"Totally," said Sturges with a nod.

The door to the technical suite opened and Detective Shoop entered followed by two uniformed officers.

"Good afternoon, Mr. Mayor. Detective Shoop, Reardon City Police," said Shoop, opening his shield and flashing it at Brewster. "I see that Dr. Barnes has explained her theory to you."

"A very interesting theory, Detective," said Brewster, "but I don't see how she can prove it."

"Actually," continued Shoop, moving further into the room, as the officers stood guard at the door, "her theory has been confirmed. The phrases on Stacy Grant's 911 tape have been verified as coming from various audio recordings. Dr. Willard Swinton, one of Dr. Barnes's colleagues, has extracted the actual splice marks on the 911 recording indicating exactly where the killer edited the recording together. Dr. Swinton tells us that the quality of the splicing is so good that the recording could only have been made on the most sophisticated of equipment. Possibly something like what you have here, Mayor."

"My people have not been involved in murder, Detective," huffed Brewster.

"That remains to be seen," observed Shoop, looking around the small room from one person to the next, his eagle eyes alert to any sign of guilt. "Certainly, everyone here had a motive. James Grant was pulling ahead in the polls, Mayor. Possibly you or one of your aides feared he'd run away with the election and your desire to win and remain in power was so great that you concocted this elaborate scheme to incriminate your opponent . . . ."

"Really, Detective," huffed Brewster, "no one on my staff would do such a thing. Besides, even if Grant got a slight uptick in the polls, we're confident in our strength to regain our support before the election . . . ."

"With strong arm tactics," suggested Pamela.

"Dr. Barnes," snapped Brewster, "I believe we've been more than gracious to you here today. And you turn around and attack us for no reason. Your Mr. Grant is the one sitting in a jail cell for murdering his own wife. That hasn't changed!"

"Actually, Mayor," noted Shoop, "I forgot to mention that we petitioned for and received a search warrant for this headquarters. While you and Mr. Baines and Mr. Sturges were here in your control room discussing fake tapes with Dr. Barnes, my men were going through your offices upstairs . . . ."

"What?" exclaimed Brewster. "You can't do that!" He surged forward. Baines and Sturges looked at each other with wide-eyed expressions.

"Harold!" shrieked Katherine, reaching for her husband to restrain him from attacking the detective. The officers at the door moved into the room but Shoop held up his hand. Pamela watched the mini-debacle play out like a movie. The whole event lasted a second but the entire room appeared to explode with emotion.

"Calm down, gentlemen," said Shoop, hands up. The officers held their hands on their weapons. "We didn't find anything."

The trio of politicians relaxed noticeably. Brewster turned and motioned for Baines and Sturges to retreat. He shook off his wife who was clinging dramatically to his arm.

"Of course, you didn't find anything, Shoop," sneered the mayor. "There's nothing to find. I hope you didn't leave our offices in a mess."

"Actually, we didn't find much of anything," continued Shoop, "except this." He removed a small tape recorder from his overcoat pocket. The expressions on the three men's faces froze. "It doesn't have much on it, but I think you'll find what it does have quite interesting." He pressed the "play" button and the recorded voice of Stacy Grant filled the small room.

'My husband . . . outside . . . trying to . . . break in. Please help!'

"That doesn't mean anything," cried Brewster as Shoop stopped the recording. "It's been playing on TV for weeks!"

"True," noted Shoop, "but this part hasn't been." He pressed "play" again. This time Stacy Grant's voice produced a different message, "Jim . . . come home . . . hurry!" Shoop stopped the recorder and looked around the room. Every face was riveted to the tiny device. "That recording is definitely the voice of Stacy Grant," he continued, "but it's not something she said to 911. Obviously, it's a message designed to get her husband James to come home. It's the call that James claims Stacy made to him at the rally which caused him to rush home—where he found her dead body. This message was sent as a call to James Grant either immediately before or immediately after the 911 call was made."

"Detective," said Katherine Brewster, "I don't see how these recordings implicate my husband. He couldn't have sent them. He was at the rally being interviewed by Ginger Cooper."

"True," noted Shoop. "We don't know how—or if--your husband is involved in Stacy Grant's death, Mrs. Brewster. This recording device was found on Mr. Sturges' desk."

"Kevin!" exclaimed Brewster.

"They're trying to frame me, Boss," cried Sturges, his hands shoved deep into his pockets, his face a mass of lines.

Shoop continued. "We have additional proof from station WRER that indicates that Mayor Brewster could not have made those calls personally, as he was engaged in the interview at the time the 911 call was made."

"And Ginger Cooper, the reporter who conducted the interview with your husband and with James Grant, confirms that, Mrs. Brewster," agreed Pamela. "She is a remarkably observant woman—a good quality to have if you're a newspaper reporter. Indeed, Ms. Cooper not only remembers the mayor's presence during the interview, she also recalls seeing James Grant leave—shortly after he received a call on his cell phone.   Not only that—she further recalls seeing Kevin Sturges leave shortly before she began interviewing the mayor which occurred maybe ten or fifteen minutes before James received his phone call."

"It's not true!" cried Sturges, backing away.

"Yes," Shoop proceeded. "We believe Mr. Sturges snuck out of the rally, drove to the Grant house, gained entrance through some excuse, and while Stacy Grant's back was turned, hit her with a candlestick from her own fireplace. Then, he quickly used her landline phone to call 911 and also to call James where he played the appropriate fake messages that he had prepared in advance in this editing suite. As soon as he made the calls, he left and returned to the rally, arriving just in time for the conclusion of the interview with the mayor. You probably didn't even notice his absence, Mayor."

"Kevin!" cried Brewster, turning to his young aide. "Why? Why would you do this?"

Kevin Sturges looked from the mayor to each person in the room. The two officers at the door were a firm guarantee that escape was impossible.   A noticeable drop in his shoulders made the young man seem half his normal size.

"I'm sorry, Boss," he whispered. "I thought it would help."

"Help?" shouted Brewster. "You killed a woman!"

Then, suddenly, his demeanor changed from defeated to furious. "She was a bitch!" snarled Sturges. Then, hands to his face, he sank to the floor in a heap, blubbering.

"I don't understand, Detective," said Katherine Brewster.

"We didn't either," explained Shoop. "But there's more to Mr. Sturges's motive for murder than just his desire to aid his employer's re-election campaign.   According to some intensive investigating by Grant's defense team, Mr. Conrad Gates was able to uncover a rather sordid tale of unrequited love during Sturges's college days."

"Yes," added Pamela to the group who were now apparently ignoring the killer sobbing uncontrollably on the floor. "Kevin Sturges and Stacy were friends in college. He evidently desired more than just friendship, but she kept him at a distance. When James Grant came on the scene, Stacy was smitten and never looked back. We surmise that, Sturges resented James for stealing Stacy away from him and has been searching ever since for ways to get back at him–and her. His anger continued to build, even as he developed his skills as a videographer and editor. When James entered the race against Brewster, it appeared to become too much of a temptation for Sturges. He saw the opportunity to remove James as a political opponent for his employer as well as an opportunity to get back at Stacy for rebuffing him those many years ago. That's when he hatched this plot. We suspect that he's been planning it for many months."

"True," added Shoop, "and we probably would have never tumbled to it, had it not been for Dr. Barnes and her group of faculty researchers who just didn't believe the sound on that 911 recording."

"So, Detective," asked Brewster cautiously, "does this affect my campaign?"

"Mayor," said Shoop with a shrug, "I have no idea how it will affect your campaign. That's not my concern. My only concern right now is informing you—Mr. Sturges—that you are under arrest for the murder of Stacy Grant. You have the right to remain silent . . . ." He continued to read Kevin Sturges his rights, as the two police officers stepped over to the young man in a heap on the floor, lifted him up, handcuffed him, and led him out of the room.

As soon as the officers and Shoop had left with Sturges, Mayor Brewster, his wife, and Victor Baines came towards Pamela.

"Dr. Barnes," said Katherine, "I don't really know what to say to you. You deceived me into letting you in here, allowing the police an opportunity to search my husband's offices. I find that offensive. On the other hand, Kevin committed a murder—a murder unjustly attributed to another person. I cannot condone his actions."

"Neither can I," said Brewster, beside his wife with his arm behind her back. "You are a bit of a snoop, Doctor, and I don't appreciate you mucking about in my business. But I had no idea what Kevin was up to. It sickens me to think he killed that poor woman—and for what?"

"He got wrapped up in the campaign," noted Victor Baines, standing behind them. "It happens. We begin to think we're infallible—that if we can manipulate voters, we can manipulate anything. We can't. We all need to stop and smell the roses. Dr. Barnes, I want to apologize to you for my behavior the other day."

Katherine and her husband glanced at Baines as he moved towards Pamela.

"You're one gutsy gal," continued Baines, shaking Pamela's hand. "If more women were like you . . . ."

"I'll second that," said Katherine with a nod and a smile. She beamed at her husband.

Chapter Thirty

This was the second time that Pamela found herself in the bowels of the Reardon City Hall–this time in the small lobby of the city's jail waiting with Willard, Joan, and Martin, with great anticipation for the release of James Grant. They all sat on very uncomfortable folding chairs lined up against the concrete walls waiting for the return of the clerk who had promised that he would check on the status of "prisoner" Grant.

She checked her watch and noted that the four of them had been sitting here for over twenty minutes.

"They said he'd be released at ten a.m.," said Martin with noticeable anxiety. "Poor guy. He gets his freedom, but he's lost his wife."

"We're all going to have to pull together to help him cope," offered Joan.

"Definitely," agreed Willard. "I hope we can convince him to stay in the race. Don't you think Stacy would have wanted him to do that?"

"I do, my friend," responded Martin, patting Willard's hand, "but he's suffered a huge loss and it just may take some time."

The door at the back of the small lobby opened and the clerk/guard entered, followed by James Grant, no longer wearing his official orange prison outfit. He was dressed in a pair of beige trousers and a light blue short-sleeve shirt, clothes Martin had delivered to him earlier. James's face was drawn and pale.

The foursome waiting for him in the lobby perked up and rose as a unit.

"James!" they all greeted him. As James moved towards them, Martin embraced his friend, and Willard, Joan, and Pamela all shook his hand.

"Let's get you out of here, buddy," said Martin, escorting a placid James up the jail stairs and into the bright outdoor sunlight. James covered his face from the glare as Martin led the group to his car.

"Wait a minute, Martin," said James, suddenly, standing in front of Martin's Toyota. "I understand I have you three to thank for my freedom." He leaned weakly against the car with Martin's arm around his back. "If it weren't for you three, I'd probably still be in jail. I don't know how you academic people manage to do these things—but I know this was above and beyond the call of duty. I just want to say, thank you."

"You're welcome, James," replied Willard.

"Of course, James," agreed Joan. "We're all in your corner and support you."

"We're glad we could use our specialties to come to your assistance," added Pamela.

"True," noted James, gathering some energy as he spoke. "But the three of you were there for me before this horrible thing happened to Stacy. You were there helping with my campaign."

"We believe in you, James," said Joan, "I've known you a long time. I understand your opposition to Hap Brewster. This community has suffered enough under his neglect."

"I couldn't argue with you," agreed James.

"James," said Willard, coyly, "I notice that you haven't removed your name from the ballot. Dare I ask if you plan to stay in the race?"

"I don't know, Willard," replied the harried-looking man. "I need to think about it. But I will promise you this. I won't remove my name from the ballot without a lot of thought."

"Wonderful!" cried Joan.

"Good," agreed Pamela. "Do give it some time."

"Besides," added Martin, giving his friend a squeeze, "I really think that Stacy would want you to stay in the race."

"I know, Martin. I know," said James, nodding. "He's been nagging me with that argument every time he visits," he added as he looked at the other three.

"I am your campaign manager," exclaimed Dobbs. "It's my job to see you get elected!"

"I don't know," mused James, arms crossed. "With Sturges gone, Brewster can probably revive his image—and, of course, we know he has tactics that will convince voters that don't involve persuasion."

"Now you're thinking like a candidate!" shouted Dobbs.

"Go, James!" cried Joan.

"Grant for Mayor!" added Pamela.

"Yippee!" concluded Willard. A general air of goodwill pervaded the little confab that had gathered beside Martin Dobbs's car.

After a few minutes, Pamela looked up and saw a van entering the parking lot. On the side of the van, the text "WRER" alerted her to the arrival of a news crew that had probably just gotten wind of Grant's release. She tapped Martin Dobbs on the shoulder and pointed to the newly arrived vehicle. Dobbs motioned for James to get in the car. Pamela, Joan, and Willard all hustled into Pamela's Civic nearby just as Ginger Cooper alighted from the passenger side of the van followed by several crew men out of the side doors.

"Mr. Grant!" yelled Cooper, running towards the departing cars. "Mr. Grant! Now that you're out of jail, are you planning to remain in the race? Can you let our viewers know, Mr. Grant?" She ran up to the passenger window of Martin's car, a videographer filming her movements.

Martin backed out of the parking space, and then stopped suddenly. James abruptly rolled down his window and leaned out and looked directly at Ginger Cooper.

"Yes, Miss Cooper," he replied. "I am thrilled to be out of jail and delighted to finally be exonerated in my wife's murder. I am more than happy that the true killer—Kevin Sturges—the mayor's communication director, has confessed, I understand." James discussed his desire to seek justice in his wife's killing. Eventually he said, "And—here's your scoop, Ginger. I will stay in this race and not only that, I will win it!"

Epilogue

It was another popcorn in bed night for Pamela and Rocky. As usual, Candide was vying for kernels as he pranced from one corner of the mattress to another, stopping every once in a while to nuzzle in between his mistress and master when they dropped a crunchy nugget between them. The late night news had just started, and as usual Pamela had turned to WRER to see Ginger Cooper deliver the bombshell of the day that James Grant had been released from jail and that he had announced that he would remain in the race for mayor.

"This has been quite a busy day for young Mr. Grant," said Rocky, stuffing a handful of popcorn in his mouth. "Gets out of jail, announces to the press that he intends to stay in the race."

"Quiet!" Pamela whispered to her husband. "I want to hear it. Maybe you'll see me. I'm off to the side."

"Behind the scenes, as usual," sighed Rocky.

The telephone rang.

"Oh, no!" cried Pamela. "Whoever it is, I can't talk. I have to see this," she ordered her husband in a hushed voice, her eyes intent on the screen at the foot of their bed. Rocky lifted the receiver and said "hello."

"WRER has an exclusive interview with James Grant, released today from jail after being accused of the bludgeoning death of his wife Stacy," announced Cooper.

"Hey, Angie!" said Rocky to their daughter on the phone line. He listened as Pamela continued to focus on Ginger Cooper on the screen.

The picture on the television changed to that of the parking lot where Ginger Cooper had acquired her brief interview with James. James looked frazzled but joyful as he spoke directly into the camera, with Ginger Cooper's microphone visible at the bottom of the picture frame.

"Mr. Grant," asked the reporter, "can you tell us your plans now that you have been cleared in your wife's death?"

James spoke for several minutes about his intentions to see justice done and Kevin Sturges convicted for his wife's murder.

"What?" cried Rocky into the phone. "What did you say?" he repeated. Pamela turned her head in response to the change in his voice. He put his hand over the receiver and looked at her. "Angie's foundation is sending her to Africa."

"What?" exclaimed Pamela. "Africa!"

"Yeah," he replied, returning immediately to the phone to listen to his daughter. Pamela was riveted to her husband's conversation with their young, inexperienced, totally unsophisticated daughter. On TV, Ginger Cooper was asking James whether or not he would stay in the mayoral race.

James replied as he had that afternoon, just as Pamela remembered it, "And—here's your scoop, Ginger. I will stay in this race and not only that, I will win it!" Pamela felt the same gratification that she had experienced earlier, knowing that she had contributed to helping this young politician make their town a better place to live. However, her joy was short-lived as her attention was drawn back to her husband's conversation with Angie. How on earth could Angie even consider going to Africa? Rocky was listening and nodding.

"What does she say?" Pamela asked Rocky, pulling on his arm in an attempt to get the phone and speak with Angie herself.

"Just a minute," he whispered to his wife, pushing her hand away. "Yes, yes," he spoke into the receiver. "Just a minute, Ang," he said into the phone, "let me explain this to your mother. She's having a small fit right now." He held the receiver down and said, "The national office of Angie's organization has selected five regional reps to send to Africa for their upcoming campaign. Angie is one of those five— from all over the country. Babe, it's a terrific honor! She'll be there for a year . . . ."

"A year!" Pamela shrieked. "A year! She's barely been on her own just across town from us. How can she possibly get along in a foreign country?"

"She has to start sometime," he argued, placing a hand calmingly on her shoulder. "Just a minute." He put the receiver back to his mouth. "Hey, Ang. Yeah, your Mom is freaking out. Oh, she worries about you—you know. Yeah, yeah. I know, but that's how mothers are. You'll just have to get used to it."

"She's not happy about this, is she?" whispered Pamela in his ear.

"Yeah, she appears to be," he responded back to his wife. "Sorry, Ang. She's chomping at the bit to talk to you. No, she'll probably try to talk you out of it. What? Me? Hey, Ang. I'm for whatever you want to do. I think it's a great opportunity!"

"What!" cried Pamela. "Rocky, she's barely twenty-one! You surely can't approve of her gallivanting all over the world all by herself."

"I don't get the impression she'll be by herself," he added to his wife. "She'll be traveling with this group of interns from her foundation, visiting the places in Africa that the foundation supports with its funding. Gee, Pammie. It sounds like a wonderful opportunity!"

"Let me talk to her," she said, grabbing for the phone. He pulled it away.

"You watch your newscast," he ordered. "Hey, Ang," he said into the phone. "Yeah, I'll calm her down. It'll all be fine. Don't worry! We're behind you, kiddo! Okay! See ya!" He hung up, glaring at Pamela.

"I need to speak to Angie," said Pamela with a scowl. Rocky glared back. She tried to grab the phone.

"You're just acting like a mother," he warned her. "Why don't you calm down a bit, then call her back. Besides, look! There's Hap Brewster!" Rocky pointed to the TV screen where Hap Brewster appeared in front of a dozen or so microphones. "Now what? Don't tell me he's going to start in on poor Grant as soon as he gets out of jail?"

"Listen," Pamela ordered Rocky with a finger to her lips.

"Fellow Reardonites," intoned Brewster in the manner Pamela had become accustomed to over the years—that folksy political style that she found demeaning. "As you all may know, my primary opponent for this office, James Grant, was recently released from jail—because he had been wrongly accused in his wife's recent murder. Wrongly, I add, because of a devious plot created by one of my campaign's top advisors—Kevin Sturges. Now, although I did not personally have any knowledge of Mr. Sturges's machinations in implicating Mr. Grant in his heinous crime, I do feel a personal responsibility that his actions led to Mr. Grant being unfairly detained—his reputation tarnished—if only temporarily. Now, Mr. Grant is a free man and has announced that he will continue in the campaign against me. I am glad to hear that this is the case. Because if he had decided to withdraw, it would have made my decision all the more difficult. You see, after a serious discussion with my wife Katherine, a very wise woman, I have decided that my political days are over—or at least, should be over. I have come to recognize Mr. Grant as a person of extreme integrity and capability—and an individual who has surrounded himself with equally fine assistants—unlike myself. Therefore, I am dropping out of the race."

Pamela froze—her eyes glued to Brewster's face on the screen. Her fist reached out and jabbed her husband's arm.

"I will continue my duties as mayor for the time being," continued Brewster, "but will work closely with Mr. Grant to assure a seamless transition come November. Finally, even though it is too late for me to officially remove my name from the ballot, I urge you all to cast your votes for James Grant for mayor—because if elected, I will not serve."

"Wow!" said Rocky, "I can't believe the guy just gave up."

"Me neither," added Pamela, "I think his wife may have had something to do with it. She struck me as a very persuasive woman."

"Sort of like you?" he asked.

"Maybe," she responded. "Who would have thought that all this would have happened? Certainly, I never would have considered it back when Joan first dragged me to James' stump speech at that rally in the park."

The couple went quiet. Eventually, Rocky looked at his wife.

"I suppose you're going to try to convince Angie to stay here in Reardon and not go to Africa?"

"No, I'm not."

"What?" he asked. "I thought you thought she was too young and inexperienced to travel alone."

"I don't know, Rocky," said Pamela, "life is short and we never know what's around the corner. Bad things happen right here in Reardon. We can't protect her everywhere. All we can do is just trust that we've raised her to be resourceful enough to take care of herself in any circumstance."

"That's my girl!" cried Rocky, giving his wife a warm embrace.

"But I don't have to like it," she added, tears streaming down her face. "She is my baby."

Candide, noticing Pamela sobbing, bounded over to his mistress and began licking her face—his doggie way of expressing concern. Rocky joined the little dog, embracing his wife warmly. The little family of three comforted and loved each other—and hugs and face licks abounded.

Rocky's Recipes

Stump Speech Stew

    1 lb. lean hamburger
    1 lb. pk. mixed frozen vegetables
    1/4 cup steak sauce
    1 cup red cooking wine
    4 cups chicken or beef broth
    1/4 cup orzo

    Sauté hamburger then add remaining ingredients and simmer for at least 30 minutes.

Politician's Pie (named so because it's mostly just a lot of hot air)

    4 egg whites
    1 tsp. vanilla
    1 tsp. vinegar
    1 cup sugar

    Beat first three ingredients in electric mixer until egg whites are stiff. Add sugar gradually until glossy. Form a crust in a greased 10-inch pie pan and bake at 275 degrees for one hour.

    When the shell is cool, it may be filled with any of a variety of fillings–pudding, ice cream, berries or other fruits. Be sure to top with whipped cream.

Stump Speech Murder is the fourth in the Pamela Barnes acoustic mystery series. The first, *Sounds of Murder*, represented Patricia Rockwell's debut novel.

Patricia Rockwell has spent most of her life teaching. Her Bachelors' and Masters' degrees are from the University of Nebraska in Speech, and her Ph.D. is from the University of Arizona in Communication. She was on the faculty at the University of Louisiana at Lafayette for thirteen years, retiring in 2007. Her publications are extensive, with over 20 peer-reviewed articles in scholarly journals, several textbooks, and a research volume published by Edwin Mellen Press. In addition, she served for eight years as editor of the *Louisiana Communication Journal*. Her research focuses primarily on deception, sarcasm, and vocal cues. Dr. Rockwell is presently living in Aurora, Illinois, with her husband Milt, also a retired educator. The couple has two adult children.